THE HOLLOW REALMS

ASHES OF THE NECROPOLIS

JORDAN ALLEN

For my beloved family.

Contents

Prologue

Nestled atop the cliffs of the Kalt mountains sat a city of stone. It was a quiet place where few ventured to and even fewer ventured from. The shining moon hung low in the sky and illuminated the city as a weary traveller strode up the stone path.

The traveller in his golden armour glistened as he walked, and his large mace swung by his side as he trod up the rocky steps that led into the city.

"Ho there, wanderer," called an old man from behind a gate, holding his grimy lantern high. So grimy in fact that you would think it wasn't lit at all. "State your name and tell me what business you have in Furcht at this time of night?"

The man in gold armour held up his hands. "My

name is Alrich, and I assure you that I mean no trouble. I have been on the road for days and am in need of a place to rest. Is that permissible?"

"Well, Master Alrich, if you require a place to rest then it is odd that you should come somewhere so out of the way. I need not tell you that considering you've climbed more than halfway up the mountain. That's no easy feat."

"It is true that I need a place to rest, but that is not my only business here."

The old man sighed and nodded. "You're here for the passageway, aren't you?"

"That I am," agreed Alrich.

"I would beg you not to enter that treacherous dungeon, Master Alrich. No good came of it a century ago and no good will come of it a century from now. I also suspect no good will come from it at any time between, including now."

"I'm afraid that I have made up my mind. If you would be so kind as to let me into the city, I will make my way there and trouble you no further."

The old man looked despondent, but he relented and waved Alrich through. The traveller opened the gate and stepped into the city as the old man slinked off to a small guardhouse without saying another word.

Alrich wandered down the street in near-complete darkness. Not a soul had a torch lit nor a lantern warming their doorstep. It was an odd place, to be sure. Alrich was well-travelled and even the smallest of villages were livelier than this at this hour. Granted, it may have been mostly rowdy drunkards and night watchmen.

No matter. The golden man walked up staircases of limestone and past walls of granite, looking for his destination. The old guard had called it the passageway, but Alrich knew it as the Necropolis of Furcht.

The Necropolis was talked about in legends for many centuries, some believing it to be a myth, but Alrich had studied the reports and accounts well. He was certain that it held the secrets of life and death. There he would finally find what he needed. The Elixir of Life.

Alrich walked in and out of alleyways, up a staircase here, down a ledge there. The city was maze-like, and it only added to Alrich's sense of unease. The journey into the depths of the Necropolis was one that few returned from and those that did return vowed never to enter again.

"It will be worth it," Alrich had muttered to himself countless times during the past few weeks on the road. "It is for my son."

The wanderer's young son was at death's door and time was of the essence. Every healer that Alrich had spoken to said the same thing. The lad had only a month or two left. The only thing that could save him was the legendary elixir.

"There it is," whispered Alrich under his breath.

At the edge of the city, built into the mountain, was an ornate archway of the finest marble, more pristine than the already well-cared-for limestone that made up most of the city. The archway was decorated with carvings of figures, from humans to dragons. The humans all stood defiantly at the top, but the creatures near the bottom were hunched and dishevelled. What lay before Alrich had matched the drawings from the old records perfectly.

Within the archway was a staircase that led

downwards into the darkness. It was a foreboding sight, there was no mistake in that. The majestic front existed solely to mask the sinister secrets held beneath.

"I am tired," sighed Alrich as he walked towards the arch. He wanted to rest, but he felt his legs moving. He did not know whether it was of his own accord or not. He suspected not, but he did not care.

Alrich grabbed his mace with his right hand and cast a spell with his left. A glowing light emitted from his palm and then circled around him. There was no time to rest, the Necropolis was calling to him.

The man in gold walked down the staircase and out of sight. Nobody but the guard had noticed him as he passed through the town. It was as though he had never come to Furcht at all.

Chapter 1

The City in the Mountainside

The dawn was cruel this morning as Erde surveyed his ransacked camp. The mountain wolves, with their once-beautiful grey fur, lay bloody and dead at his feet. The mercenary knew that he had little time before other predators smelled the blood. He must leave and he must leave soon.

Erde packed the rest of his gear, kicked the wolf bodies off the edge of the cliff and pressed ahead. The previous night's chill was in the air and he was hungry. The city that lay ahead would doubtlessly have bread and fresh meat for sale. As tempting as it was to tear some flesh from the wolves for a cookout, now was not the time to satiate his appetite.

The traveller continued up the mountain path,

his auburn hair glistening in the rising sun. Patches of rough grass sparkled with dew as they overlooked the jagged rocks that lay below and the badlands that stretched towards the horizon.

It had been a long week on the road and Erde was used to having three or four travelling companions accompanying him. Sadly, they had all journeyed to the city of Furcht without him. Erde understood it, of course, he had been bedridden and barely conscious for the past three months. What use was he?

Erde glanced at his leg. It was covered by cloth and metal, but he knew the sight of the mangled mess that lay beneath. It had been healed by the might of Saint Wilhelm and with the grace of the True One, but the scars would remain. He was lucky to still have the leg at all. In fact, he was lucky to be alive.

Climbing the stone staircase, Erde reached a rusty iron gate. The guardhouse past the gate lay abandoned, the wooden door having long been removed. The mercenary pushed the gate open and walked into the city.

Furcht was a magnificent place, a true work of human ingenuity. It was as beautiful as it was old. Once a monastery for worshippers of Mallabeth, god of the undead, it was raided by barbarians who forced the necromancers out and claimed it as their own. The barbarians built endlessly and it became a serene haven, out of reach for the lazy and too fortified for invading evil.

Erde walked down the street, looking for signs of life. In his home city of Olfen, a similar street would be bustling with activity. Traders looking to sell their wares, farmers carting food into town, and the occasional pickpocket hoping to make a quick coin without losing their fingers.

"Marnin'," came a gruff voice from an open door to the left. A bald man with a black beard and scraggy clothing was staring at Erde.

"Greetings," said Erde.

"It's not often I see strangers about," said the man. "Name's Garz, and you?"

"Erde of Olfen," said Erde, raising his fist to his chest in salute.

"You're here for the passageway?"

"No, what is that?"

Garz narrowed his eyes in suspicion. "Every unfortunate soul who comes to Furcht comes here for the passageway. The Dungeons of Kalt. The Necropolis. Whatever name you want to use for it. I find it very hard to believe that a man who looks like you is not here to seek the passageway. Am I wrong?"

Erde was confused. "I assure you that I have never heard of such a place. I'm here looking for my companions. I was told that they ventured to Furcht and that was all I had to go on. I had not heard of your town until a week ago. I know nothing about any passageways or dungeons. That is a promise, Garz."

Garz burst into laughter. It was a raucous laughter and Erde wasn't sure how much of it was exaggerated. It got on his nerves, nonetheless. Garz continued laughing for almost a minute before calming down.

"I'm sorry, Erde," said Garz, wiping tears from his eyes. "Nobody comes here without knowing about the passageway. It could be warriors in search of a challenge, mages in search of magic, or even a peasant in search of a few coins. You're special, you are."

"I don't appreciate you mocking me, Garz," said Erde sternly. "I shall take my leave before I do something I regret. May we never cross paths again. Farewell."

"Come now," said Garz, suddenly more composed. "I meant nothing by it. You can't deny an old soul like me a little laughter in a place as bleak as this, right? Tell me of your friends, perhaps I saw 'em passing through. I see a lot of things from this doorway."

Erde stared at Garz coldly, not in the mood for any more nonsense, but he relented. "Their names are Troyes, Heidi, Waren and Fueur. They would have arrived a few weeks ago, perhaps two months at most?"

"I'm afraid that isn't ringing any bells, but I don't always ask the names when I spot newcomers around here. What did they look like?"

Erde sensed this would be a fruitless conversation. "Troyes is a tall, burly fellow, usually adorned with animal skin. He towers above everybody else. Heidi is a fair woman with blonde hair, very beautiful, but often covered by a cloak when travelling. Waren is a sorcerer and makes no secret of it, he would stand out a mile off. Fueur is a tall man and often wears his shining armour, even on the road. Cumbersome, but we can't talk him out of it."

"That last one sounds somewhat familiar. Does he wield a big sword with a gold hilt and glowing blade?"

Erde was suddenly more engaged. "Yes. Yes, that's him. You've seen him? Please tell me every detail."

Garz began to shake his head slowly and scratch his beard. "I don't know what to tell you, Erde. He went straight for the passageway, and I haven't seen him since. That's not unusual when people go there. It would have been nearly two months ago, much like you said. It's as I told you, everybody who comes to Furcht makes their way there."

"Where is this passageway? If that's where my friends are, then that's where I must go."

"You don't want to go there, trust me on this," said Garz, looking very serious.

"Why?"

"It's rare that those who venture through ever return. In the passageway, you need no food, you need no rest, and you most definitely need to hold onto every last fibre of your sanity if you want to make it out alive. It's a cursed place, nowhere like it exists across the entire Outer World."

"If you would give me directions, I would appreciate it," said Erde, his mind already made up.

"There is nothing I can do to persuade you otherwise?"

"I'm afraid not, Garz. If I knew I was going to my doom, I would still have to go. I must find them."

Garz let out a long sigh. "Head deeper into the town and take a left at the town square. Keep walking as if you were going towards the path up the mountain and you'll find it. Huge archway, you can't miss it."

"Thank you," said Erde as he resumed walking. "I'm sure that we will meet again when I return with my companions."

"I'll be here," said Garz solemnly. "Old Garz is always here."

The mercenary walked towards the square and did not see a single soul. He was convinced that he spotted a small child spying on him from a window, but when he looked again there was nobody there. The eeriness of the lonely, run-down town was accentuated by the light coating of mist that obscured some of the more distant buildings.

In the centre of the town square were the remains of a water fountain. The stone border reached Erde's waist and in the centre of the fountain, standing atop a pedestal, was a statue of a man. He wore a loose tunic and held a large egg in his hand. The pool beneath the statue was filled to the brim with dirty water, mixed with dead leaves and grime. Whatever drain that sat at the bottom of the fountain had been clogged for some time.

Erde continued to follow Garz's directions, and his stomach began to growl. How he wished he had cooked one of the wolves from this morning. Garz's words about not needing food in the Necropolis rang in his head. What did the stranger mean by this? Perhaps it was stupid of Erde to press on without learning more about this passageway.

As the mercenary climbed one of the many stone staircases in the city, he turned back to look down upon Furcht from this new height. It was as empty as it had been when he passed through previously. Something was wrong, but he could not put his finger on it. He had to be sensible and check.

Erde walked back down the staircase and through the town, searching for Garz. The

Necropolis could wait a few minutes. It was going nowhere.

"Garz?" called Erde as he approached the doorway where the man had once stood.

There was no answer.

Erde walked inside the house and began to cough. It was incredibly dusty as though nobody had been here for decades. He scanned around and furrowed his brow in confusion. Perhaps nobody had been here for decades?

He rummaged through the rooms, opening all of the cupboards and drawers, trying to find some semblance of life. There was none. The clothes in the cupboard were old, the drawers were empty, and the food had since long-rotted away based on the stained wood on the kitchen surfaces. Nobody had lived here for many, many years.

"An old soul indeed," uttered Erde, remembering what Garz had said. "I suppose there is nothing else for it..." He departed from Garz's house and began the walk back to the town square to resume his climb.

As Erde walked, he did not truly understand why he was continuing. The draw of finding his companions was strong, but there was something more. He knew that it was a dangerous idea and that such a large city would not be abandoned for no reason. Whatever ghost or apparition that Garz was, he had made it very clear that the Necropolis was not a place you were likely to return from. It was as though he was being called to enter by an unseen force. A force preying upon his desire to find his friends.

"This must be it," said Erde as he walked towards the archway in the mountainside. He did not stop to survey the figures carved into the stone.

Erde walked down the staircase and into the darkness. He couldn't see a thing, so he squatted in the dark stairway and drew a torch from his bag. He raised his right hand and cast the only spell he knew, Spark.

Sparks emitted in a small flurry from his fingertips and the cloth adorning the torch caught fire. Waren had tried to teach Erde many pyromancy spells, but Erde did not have the patience for it. This trick, however, had come in very handy many times over and it was because of Fueur's insistence that he took Waren up on his offer to learn it.

"If you are capable of learning a useful spell, why wouldn't you? It may just save your life," Fueur had always said. He was right, of course, but Erde wouldn't tell him that.

At the bottom of the staircase stood a door. It was made of a heavy stone and was covered almost entirely by skeletal hands. They twitched as Erde approached. Erde used the hilt of his sword to push on the door, careful to avoid the hands. It was not going to move.

One of the hands beckoned the mercenary forward and Erde found himself reluctantly moving towards it. He was now certain of it. He was under the thrall of the Necropolis. It was trying to pull him inside on its terms, not his own. He tried to pull himself away, but the skeletal hands lunged forward and grabbed him tightly.

The door began to open as Erde struggled and was dragged inside. All went black for a moment and his gut felt like it was trying to leap upwards and out of his throat. He was suddenly pushed

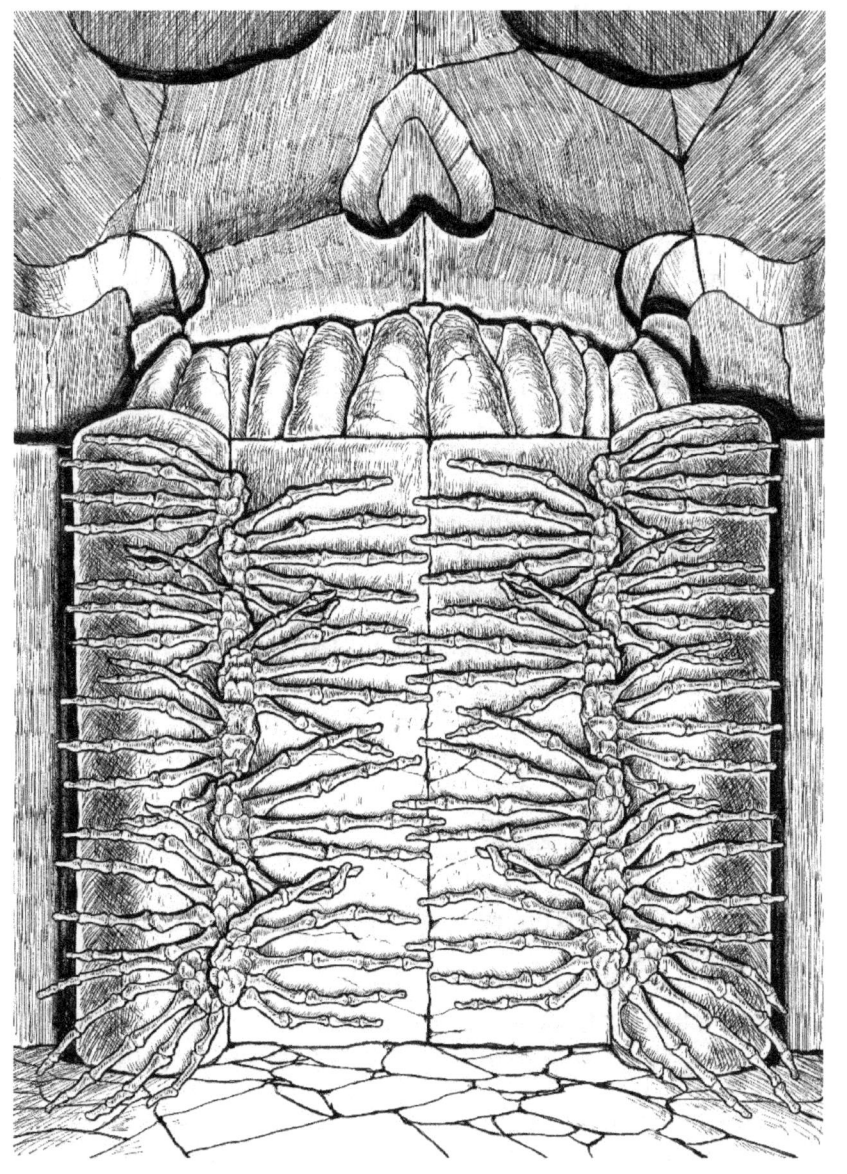

away by the skeletal hands and fell to the ground awkwardly.

He was on the other side of the door, but he was...still where he entered from? Erde picked up his torch from the floor and held it above his head. He was in the exact same passageway. He looked towards the door and found that it was as before, covered by the skeletal hands.

Erde jammed the hilt of his sword into the hands, but they were impervious to his thumps. There was not a twitch or flinch from them. They did not react at all. He tried pushing the door and it would not budge. He was locked in here with no idea of how to escape.

He knew it was useless to continue bashing on the door and that his friends were here somewhere. There was nothing else for it but to find them and figure out the puzzle together.

The mercenary climbed the staircase and found himself standing underneath the archway once more. There was a heavy fog in the air and Erde could barely see ten feet in front of himself. The chilly morning air was now a numbing cold in the absence of the sun's rays.

Erde extinguished his torch and walked towards the centre of town, his sword readied. The houses were as they were before, forebodingly quiet. The mercenary trod carefully, unsure of his surroundings.

"Grruuuh," came a low rumble as a clumsy hand struck at Erde.

The mercenary whipped his blade upwards and cut the hand off at the wrist, sending it hurtling through the air. Erde brought his blade back down in a swift motion and cut the head from his attacker.

The head's former owner was a hunched man, slightly smaller than Erde. He lay sprawled on the ground, his clothes ragged and his skin a sickly grey. He was both scrawny and bloated, and physically revolting in every way. A ghoul.

Another ghoul charged at Erde through the fog and Erde felt its strong grip on his shoulder. He rammed his elbow into its neck, but it gripped even tighter. Drawing a knife from his belt, he thrust it over his shoulder and into the creature's eye socket as it was about to bite down on his flesh. The undead abomination was deceased once more.

Erde looked around quickly, trying to work out where he was. He ran to the side, hoping to find shelter. He clumsily collided with a rickety wooden door and barged his way inside.

The fog was still in the air, even inside the small stone house, but it was thin enough to see more clearly. Erde slammed the door closed and began to move the old furniture in front of it, hoping to buy himself a moment of peace and some time to think of a plan.

The mercenary began to chuckle to himself. He was no stranger to fights with monsters, both natural and unnatural, but this would be his first real test since his recovery. Wolves were child's play, but an army of ghouls in a dense fog would be a fun challenge.

At least one ghoul began to ram on the door, followed by another, then a third at the window. Erde's brief moment of peace was over. He opened the window and jammed his sword through it, killing the ghoul, before closing the window again. The door was loose and collided repeatedly with the kitchen table that Erde had propped against it.

"Come on," he whispered, waiting for the ghouls to break through.

Seconds later, the table was forced backwards and, not two, but five ghouls charged into the room. Erde neatly cut the head from the first and kicked the corpse into the second ghoul. The third ghoul pounced on him, knocking him to the ground. The fourth and fifth piled on top, each grabbing at him and trying to take a bite of his flesh.

Erde wrestled his arm free and pierced the skull of the third ghoul with his knife. He held his hand to the face of the fourth ghoul, careful not to lose a finger, and cast Spark. The ghoul was blinded, but it did little good. It was already on top of him.

The mercenary mustered all of his strength and threw the pile of undead aside. He rolled aside and stood up, ready to strike with his sword. The two remaining ghouls charged at him. Erde swung his blade, cutting both of their heads from their bodies with a single sweep.

He tried to catch his breath, but another ghoul charged into the room. Erde dispatched it quickly and ran up the stairs. He pushed the bed in front of the door and leaned against the wall. He was tired but otherwise unscathed.

Chuckling once more, he walked over to the window and peered out. It didn't look like there were any ghouls immediately below, but he couldn't see far enough to know for sure if the cost was clear.

Sitting on the ground, Erde tried to piece together what had happened when he passed through the stone door. Was he in the same Furcht or an alternate world? Garz had called it the passageway, perhaps he meant the door was the way into this version of Furcht. Was it only Furcht or was it the entirety of the Kingdom of Kalmere?

As Erde pondered his theories, his ears pricked up. A large stomping sound echoed in the distance as the house vibrated with each of the steps. What manner of creature could cause this?

The stomping grew louder and Erde stealthily gazed from the window hoping to see whatever was approaching. He prayed it was not coming for him.

A hulking shadow, at least ten feet tall appeared in the fog. Its features were murky, but Erde could make out four large tusks protruding from its lower jaw, two short and two long. Its saucepan-sized hands ended in pointed claws that would easily tear a man in half. As it emerged from the fog, Erde could see its hairy head and the pus-filled boils that covered its body. This creature was no mere ghoul.

It was going to walk right beneath Erde's window, so he crouched low. If the creature looked up, he was a dead man.

The stomping stopped and Erde held his breath. The pig-like monster grunted and snorted, causing the glass in the window to rattle. After a long five seconds had passed, it continued forwards and away from the window. A short while later, the stomping had faded away and Erde was seemingly alone once more.

Chapter 2

The Guardhouse

The soft wind created a draft in the empty house. It travelled up the staircase, under the door and into the bedroom. It awakened Erde from his daze and he began to unblock the door, finally daring to venture outside again.

In truth, he was not afraid of death. He was afraid of not finding his companions. He would prefer to find them alive, of course, but he would reluctantly settle for learning of an unfortunate fate.

The mercenary walked down the street, keeping his sword tightly gripped with both hands. His weak fiery cantrip would be of no use to him here for the undead could not feel the same pain as a living being. It seemed obvious in hindsight, but it was a lesson learned.

Erde froze as footsteps approached. There was no mistaking the sound of the clunk of a heavy boot hitting the cobblestones. It was no ghoul, but it was no pig monster.

"Another wanderer? My, oh, my," came a man's voice.

"Show yourself," demanded Erde.

"There's no need for hostility, friend," came the voice as its owner walked through the fog and into view.

He stood before Erde, of similar height and well-built. He wielded a mace and wore a tarnished set of gold armour that had seen better days, but his most curious feature was his helmet.

The top was pointed like a crown, but the front of the helmet was mask-like, with the face being that of a happy expression. Erde could see more faces on the sides of his helmet, with the helmet face on the man's left side bearing a sad expression. On his right, the helmet showed a neutral expression.

Erde was in no mood for pleasantries. "If you've been here for longer than five minutes, I'm sure you'll understand why I'm on edge."

The man let out a small chuckle. "I've been here for longer than you've been alive, stranger. You'll have to forgive me for finding joy in meeting somebody who isn't trying to kill me. You must never take moments like these for granted when one's entire existence consists of maintaining one's sanity."

"You've been trapped here for decades?" asked Erde, not believing what he had just heard.

"You get used to it," said the man as his helmet

rotated of its own accord to the neutral expression. What was once the back of his helmet was now at the side, revealing an angry expression.

Erde was caught off guard by the helmet's movement. "What was that?"

"What was what?"

"Your helmet?"

"Oh, I see," chuckled the man, his helmet rotating to the happy expression once more. "It's quite magnificent, isn't it? It's why they call me the Man with Four Faces."

Erde did not see any point in dwelling of the nature of this bizarre fellow. Furcht itself was of a much greater concern to him. "Is the entire world like this? Are we in a parallel plane?"

"That would be telling," said the Man with Four Faces, shaking one of his fingers back and forth. "If you're fortunate enough to survive a short while, you will work it out for yourself."

"Is there anything you can tell me that will help me?" asked Erde, growing frustrated.

"That depends on what you want to know. I will give you three questions and three honest answers. Should you happen upon me again, I will give you a fourth. If we see each other a third time, a fifth. I'm sure you get the idea."

What sort of game was this? Erde wanted to cut the man's head from his body as though he were one of the ghouls, but he held back his temper. "Fine."

"Ask me anything. I am an open book at this moment in time."

"I'm looking for my companions. There are four of them: Troyes, Heidi, Waren and Fueur. I know that they came this way and I am certain that at least Fueur made it here. Do you know if any of them are still alive?"

The man raised a finger to his chin and paused before answering. "Yes."

"Where can I find them?"

"That would be four separate answers, I'm afraid. That still counts as one of your questions. Pick one name and I will tell you where I last happened upon them."

Erde clenched his fist, resisting the temptation to break his knuckles on the man's metal helmet. The man had inadvertently implied that all four had indeed made it to Furcht. Erde thought long and hard before asking his next question, debating which of his companions he would seek out first.

"Where can I find my friend, Troyes?" asked Erde, knowing he would be the best one to have by his side while seeking the others. It was very tempting to choose Heidi, but she would understand.

"Now that is indeed a good question," said the man, his helmet settling on the happy face. "Troyes is currently in the underground prison cells beneath the guardhouse at the western side of the city."

"Is that all the information you will give me?"

"I'm afraid that I've answered the three questions I offered you, my friend," said the Man with Four Faces as he took a short bow. "I look forward to our next meeting and I hope you think of a good question for me. I would very much like it if you caught me off guard, that would be most entertaining."

The golden stranger took his leave without saying another word. He faded into the fog, leaving

Erde standing alone in the haunted city once again.

The mercenary wandered westwards, hoping that the guardhouse would stand out. He had no desire to spend days in this realm, never mind the decades that the Man with Four Faces claimed to have spent. Perhaps that amount of time here would make him equally as weird. A dreadful prospect.

Every so often, a lone ghoul would approach Erde from the fog. They were of little threat by themselves, Erde having faced far tougher humans and monsters in his line of work, but he remained cautious in case the noise drew more.

Where could it be? Erde roamed the streets and alleyways trying to find the guardhouse. The fog was certainly not making things any easier. The mercenary wandered so far west that he found himself at the entrance to the city.

In the city streets, it was difficult to see more than ten feet ahead. Along the stone pathway, the fog was so thick that it appeared to be almost solid. Erde grabbed a loose pebble from the ground and tossed it into the fog. It did not ding or clink, but it fell back onto the path as though it had hit a solid sheet of iron.

Erde didn't think escaping from the city would be so easy, but he was glad he could rule out one of his theories. He climbed the stone staircase again and walked through the gate.

A loud stomp rumbled close by. It grew louder by the second, much faster than it was when Erde had last heard it. The pig was nearby. Had it been drawn to the fog wall by Erde's pebble? It must be the guardian of the city.

Erde ran inside a house and crouched low,

hoping to slip past the beast when it passed. The fast stomps drew near and Erde looked outside, trying to catch a glimpse of its route. Perhaps it was not hunting for those seeking to escape and it was an unlucky coincidence?

It was right outside. Erde watched as the towering shadow passed through the fog. It threw open the gate and walked down the path, fading out of sight quickly. It was definitely on watch; this was not merely bad luck as he had hoped.

The pig grunted and sniffed loudly, before turning back and retreating. As it passed, Erde leapt out from the shadows and slashed the beast's leg. It roared a monstrous roar and spun around, swiping at Erde. The nimble mercenary rolled out of the way and backed away from his foe.

The pig beast dropped down on all fours and charged at Erde, who dove through an open doorway as the pig collided with the wall. It stood up and roared. It was not a normal roar, bearing an unnatural hiss. If a swine made that sound back home, the local priest would be called.

Erde ran up the staircase and looked out the window. The monster stood below, staring up at him. It was calm and made no attempts to attack. Erde stared back at it, waiting for it to make a move, but it waited just as patiently. What was that roar?

As if to answer his question, a horde of ghouls appeared from the fog and barbed their way down the street. They made a variety of gruesome squelches, grunts and grumbles as they forced their way into the house and up the stairs towards Erde.

The mercenary took a deep breath, knowing he

stood no chance here, and jumped from the window and onto the street below. The pig clawed at him with his large nails, scraping Erde's side.

Erde narrowly avoided the pig's attempt to grapple him and sprinted off into the fog. The ghouls and the beast were close behind, he could hear them. The murky outlines of buildings passed him by, but he dared not risk hiding.

A ghoul pounced from the front, drawn in by the noise. Erde threw it aside with no time to finish it off. Attacking the pig was a foolish mistake. He had nowhere safe to retreat and no allies to aid him.

Erde stopped dead. The guardhouse. How could he be so stupid? He had walked past it on the way into the city and twice more a few minutes ago. Erde began to run again and started to weave through the alleys, hoping to draw the ghouls away from the main street.

The mercenary ran fast, his legs and lungs burning, but he had no choice. His scarred leg was holding up far better than he expected. As Erde rounded one of the corners, the pig stood to face him. It was smarter than he realised. It lowered its head and charged at Erde, both sharp claws raised. Erde was too tired to dodge and took the full weight of the brute.

The beast was on top of him, ready to deal the final blow, but he grabbed his knife from his belt and jammed it into the monster's chest. It yelled in anger, climbing to its feet. It pulled the knife out and tossed it aside as Erde righted himself.

The ghouls were closing in so Erde had to act fast. He ran at the pig, who aimed to charge once more. Erde threw a small burst of sparks at its face, making the beast recoil for a moment. The mercenary sprinted past, grabbing his knife along the way, and ran towards the gate once more; the pig and the ghouls still following close behind.

There it was. The guardhouse. Erde ran inside and turned his head furiously, looking for cover. A cellar door. Erde ripped open the wooden door and climbed inside, pulling it shut behind him. He waited with his sword raised, expecting the door to be ripped open and an army of ghouls to pounce upon him, but they did not come. The grumblings faded away and the pig's stomps grew distant. He was safe for now.

He used small bursts of sparks to light the way as he descended the dark staircase, but could feel his magic draining quickly. No, he must conserve it for when he needed it most, Erde pulled out his torch and lit it once more. Light filled the dark passage and the tunnels were illuminated by the orange glow.

The path ahead was murky and foreboding, even with the torchlight. The dark stone walls were a big contrast to the light stone in the city above. Whoever built this place wanted being locked down here to be a severe punishment.

Erde sat for a short while to get his breath back before proceeding deeper into the tunnels. It was not long before he spotted a small glimmer of light ahead. He approached cautiously, expecting more enemies to show themselves, and could see that the source was a barred window inside an empty, locked prison cell. It seemed to be safe here.

He gazed outside and could see only thick fog. In the normal world, perhaps this would have sat at the side of the mountain, staring into the beauty behind. A torturous reminder of wide-open space when you're trapped in a claustrophobic box.

Erde sought more cells, looking for any sign of Troyes. Most of the cells were either empty or contained the dead. Thankfully, these dead were no longer walking.

"Why did you come here?" asked a familiar voice from within a cell.

It was Troyes. The Man with Four Faces was as reliable as he was infuriating. There sat one of Erde's fellow mercenaries on the stone floor. Troyes the outlander had long brown hair and dark eyes. He was a tall man with a muscular physique who wore an unusual mixture of leather armour and animal furs.

"I have always wanted to live in a city of undead, surely I have mentioned it?" joked Erde, pleased to see his friend.

"This is no laughing matter," said Troyes. "Now you are trapped in here with us."

Erde thought Troyes would have been more grateful to be rescued. "You appear to be the trapped one, Troyes."

"You are trapped in a larger cage. You should not have followed, Erde. How did you come this far with your mangled leg?"

"The priests worked divine wonders. My leg is fully functional, but very ugly. My wife will not be happy when she sees it."

Troyes smiled for the first time, before looking sullen once again. "I'm glad to see you're okay, my friend."

"Why did the four of you leave?" asked Erde. "You all abandoned us."

"No," said Troyes, his deep voice now very soft, "we did not."

"Explain it to me," said Erde. "I'm all ears."

Troyes sighed. "Fueur was the one who abandoned everybody and the three of us followed to bring him back. He left, only telling Waren of his intent to travel here. He said that the True One had spat on him and he was risking it all on his last remaining option."

"Last remaining option for what?"

"Waren would not tell us. Weeks after Fueur left, the three of us followed, and Heidi left the little ones in her mother's care. Waren had researched heavily what this place was and he insisted that we leave you a letter warning you not to follow us," Troyes shook his head, looking ashamed of himself. "It was my fault that you followed us because I added to the letter before leaving it by your bedside."

"You were the one who scrawled the location onto the letter?"

"Yes. I did that because I thought that if you knew where we had gone, you would know that we would return. It was naïve of me. I can only apologise for being such an utter fool and leading you into this mess. I should know you well enough to know that you would try and track us down."

"Did you find Fueur? Where is Heidi? Where is Waren?" demanded Erde.

"Do not speak to me like an enemy, Erde."

"I'm sorry, my friend. It has been a trying time for me, as I'm sure it has been for you."

Troyes nodded. "We did not find Fueur. We were all separated in the city when we were hit by a horde of ghouls. Stealth is your friend in this place, particularly with the Pig Warden above. I take it you've met him?"

"Sadly, yes. He's a tough bastard to face."

"He's the one who locked me up here. He patrols the streets above, looking for anybody alive so that he can lock them in these cells. For what reason, I do not yet know."

"How long have you been in here?"

Troyes turned to the wall and counted the etchings he had made. "If time works in here the same way it does in our realm, then I've been here nearly seven weeks. No food, no water and barely a wink of sleep."

"Yet you're alive and not crazy?"

"I feel hunger, yet I do not need food. I thirst for water more than I have in my life, yet I am still alive. I do not know what magic keeps this place going, but it is powerful and it is evil. The fact that my mind is intact is a miracle in itself. Praise Belgor."

"How can I break you free?" asked Erde as he tugged on the metal door.

"One of the Pig Warden's nails is the key. You will need to either kill him and amputate his hand or...well, perhaps you can get lucky and just amputate his hand and run for it. If it were me, I would kill him."

"If you could kill him, you wouldn't be trapped in here."

Troyes let out a grim laugh. "I've missed you, Erde. If you can free me, we will find the rest of our band together."

"I will be back soon, Troyes," said Erde.

Troyes nodded. "I don't doubt it, my friend."

Erde departed, leaving his companion in the cell. He walked back the way he came, determined that he would succeed in killing the Pig Warden.

His friend's sanity and very life depended on it.

Chapter 3

Trial of the Catacombs

Emerging from the cellar, Erde stashed his torch away and drew his blade once again. Peering out from the open door frame, the streets appeared quiet. The Pig Warden and the ghouls were long gone, nowhere to be seen.

"Did you find your friend?" came a voice from behind Erde.

Erde swung his sword around at the voice and the Man with Four Faces raised his mace to block the attack.

"Be careful," said the man with a happy face, "you could put somebody's eye out swinging a sword so recklessly."

"Then I would suggest not sneaking up on people who are justifiably on edge."

The man's helmet changed to a neutral face. "That is a fair comment."

Erde lowered his weapon. "Yes, I found him. I need to find the Pig Warden to open the cell."

"Ah," said the man. "You already know where the key is then. I could help you find him if you'd simply ask the question."

"No," said Erde. "I should have no trouble finding him. What I need is a way to deal with the fog. How can I see through the fog?"

"Now you are thinking like a true denizen of Furcht," said the man as he pointed to a silver amulet around his neck. It held an aquamarine that sparkled like a serene, crystalline lake. A beautiful little trinket. "This is what you need."

"I know you will not simply give that to me," said Erde.

"No, I will not. I also need to be able to see through the fog. It is not simply through good fortune that I am still alive, although good fortune does not hurt. You can find another of these amulets in the Cathedral of the True One. There are likely others, but they will be much harder to retrieve."

"That was very generous of you," said Erde, surprised the Man with Four Faces gave up the information willingly.

"I empathise with your plight. I am not a sadist," said the man, seeing the look on Erde's face.

"I will make for the cathedral at once. You're welcome to join me."

"No thank you, friend," said the golden wanderer as he walked past Erde, through the door and into the streets. He disappeared into the fog without a trace once again.

All that Erde could think about was how strange a fellow that man was. The decades of entrapment had worn away his sanity. No matter, Erde had business to attend to.

He crept through the town, sticking close to the walls, seeking the Cathedral of the True One. The god of gods would surely have the largest building in Furcht. It should be hard to miss if that was the case, even with the fog.

Erde happened upon several ghouls as he traversed the city. Wherever there was an opportunity, he snuck up on one and impaled it with his sword. If he was at risk of getting caught, he ignored them and kept moving.

The sun was beginning to set, wherever the sun was. It was hard to tell whether the time passed the same way here as it did back home, but Erde guessed that it did remembering the days Troyes had counted on his cell wall.

As night fell upon Furcht, Erde finally found the cathedral. He was certain that he had passed it at least twice already, but missed it through the fog. Regardless, he was relieved to have shelter from the punishing streets. He did not fear the undead, but facing a horde in the night did not sound appealing. Perhaps this would be a good refuge for the night.

The grand wooden doors opened slowly, heavy as they were. Erde shut them behind himself and looked around the cathedral. It was truly magnificent.

The stained-glass windows depicting saints still glowed from the little light left outside and the pews were so many that half of the former city residents would have fit inside with ease. A statue of a winged angel sat at the furthest side of the hall. All depictions of the True One were forbidden by the church and angels often stood in his place as a representative for his glory.

Erde knelt down out of respect. He was not a devout follower of the True One, but he thought that maybe he ought to be at a time like this. After saying a short prayer, he arose and walked over to the torches adorning the wall. He poured a small amount of oil on them and ignited three of them with his Spark spell, depleting the last of his magical energy.

The mercenary roamed the hall, searching high and low for the amulet that the Man with Four Faces spoke of. He knew he was looking for a silver amulet with an aquamarine. He carried a torch with him, hoping the gem would catch the light and reveal its location.

"You there," muttered a smarmy voice from somewhere up above.

Erde looked up to see a man of around forty years old staring down at him from a balcony. He had a shaved head and a pointed face. What was most peculiar was the man's smile. He didn't look relieved to see another person, he looked utterly gleeful.

"Hail, stranger," asked Erde, giving a small salute.

"What's a fella like you doing in a city like this? Treasure hunting, are we? There are easier ways than that."

Erde didn't want to give an honest answer to a man who looked deceitful to the core. "There are easier ways, but few as thrilling as a place like this."

"I like you already, eh?" laughed the man. "Name's Alvaro. What's yours?"

"Erde of Olfen," said Erde. What harm was a name?

"Well, Erde of Olfen," muttered Alvaro. "Have I got a job for you? You can help me out and earn a few silvers for your troubles. That'll add nicely to whatever little horde you've amassed. Are you interested?"

"I'm afraid that I cannot spare the time, Alvaro. I'm seeking a very specific treasure and I cannot be delayed."

Alvaro nodded knowingly and pulled a silver amulet out from his leather armour. "One of these?"

Erde's eyes widened. "Yes. Can I convince you to part with it? I will trade you seventy silver pieces for it."

"You'll have to quadruple that, then quadruple it again," laughed Alvaro. "These things are worth a lot more than mere coins in a place like this."

Erde could see where this was going. "What is your task?"

"Now yer talkin'," said Alvaro, clapping his hands slowly. "My best mate, Eburhard, has gotten himself into a spot of bother in the catacombs below. You know how Lochmerians can be, right? There are a few undead in the way and I'm not much of a fighter in tight spaces. I prefer archery if I'm honest." Alvaro tapped a crossbow slung over his back. "If you can rescue him, the amulet is yours. I won't even ask for any of those shiny silver pieces from you. How's that for fair, eh?"

"I will see it done," said Erde. "Just point me to the entrance."

"I like you, Erde. You get straight to the point."

Alvaro pointed to a descending staircase near the cathedral doors. It was large enough to fit three men side by side and led to a pair of double wooden doors, much like smaller versions of the ones to enter the cathedral.

"I will be back shortly," said Erde as he grabbed a torch and descended the staircase.

"I'll be right here," giggled Alvaro.

The man was clearly up to something, but Erde wanted the amulet. He was no murderer, so he would try Alvaro's way first. If Alvaro played any games then Erde would deal with him and take the amulet by force. He cursed Furcht and its inhabitants under his breath as he pushed open the doors.

The tunnel ahead was dark, lit only by Erde's torch. The walls were lined with skulls and stone coffins. Not an unusual sight, but Erde did not trust them considering the undead above.

Erde leapt backwards as he rounded a corner. A group of three robed skeletons wielding longswords stood facing him from an alcove. He had his sword drawn and ready, waiting for them to make a move. They stood still, even thirty seconds later.

Letting out a low laugh, the mercenary continued past them and deeper into the catacombs. Most of the tunnels looked the same and there were many more skeletons below, each brandishing its own sword as though ready to strike.

What was that? Erde flinched as the sound of a rattle echoed down the corridor. He looked back and could not see anything out of the ordinary. Not wanting to take any chances, he retraced his steps.

Something was missing. One of the skeletons in the previous corridor was no longer standing in its alcove. Erde knew something was amiss and bashed the remaining skeletons to pieces, stomping on their skulls until they were dust.

Erde heard the whoosh of robes and the rattling of bones. He swiftly blocked an incoming attack from the missing skeleton as it pounced from the shadows. It traded a half dozen strikes with the mercenary, who then handily cleaved it in half, tearing through its tattered robes.

The skeleton lay on the ground in two pieces, but still fighting. Its upper half reached back before lunging forward to stab Erde, who kicked the sword aside and stomped on its skull.

Erde continued down the tunnels, taking the time to smash each skeleton he passed. Occasionally, one would try and fight back, but they were weak. Alvaro was a wimp if he could not best them.

As he walked past a barred hole in the wall, Erde peered through. There was a man sprawled across the floor beside a large pit. The skeletal remains of a giant stood over him. He hoped he was not too late and dashed further down the maze of tunnels, trying to find the right path.

A tunnel ahead opened into a larger room. This was it. Erde halted, waiting for the giant skeleton to make a move. The man below was as motionless as the giant. He wore black armour with a gold trim, his face obscured by a grill. This must be Eburhard.

Erde yanked a skull from the wall and tossed it into the centre of the room. The giant stood still. It was watching and waiting, ready to strike the second Erde approached. He knew it.

Creeping forward slowly, Erde refused to take his eyes away from the giant. He stood right underneath it and was ready to dash at the slightest hint of movement.

Suddenly from behind, a click followed by a whoosh.

"Argh!" yelled Erde as a bolt pierced his shoulder.

The man on the ground sat up and grabbed Erde around the waist. He flung the mercenary backwards with impressive night, throwing him into the empty pit below.

"Got him!" yelled Alvaro before bursting into laughter.

"Another fool for the pile," chuckled Eburhard as he climbed to his feet and patted the leg of the inanimate giant skeleton.

Erde lay bleeding at the bottom of the pit, twenty feet down. It was a small stone chamber and there was no easy way back up. It was a trap the whole time. How could he have been so foolish? He knew Alvaro was up to something, but the giant skeleton caught him off guard.

Alvaro looked down at him from the upper chamber. "Sorry about this, lad. We've got to earn a living, right?"

"How does my being here help you?" grunted a pained Erde, struggling to sit up. "You couldn't do me the courtesy of mugging me and being done with it? Why throw me into this pit?"

"You have two choices," said Eburhard jovially. "The first is to wait here until we grow impatient, then kill you for your things. The second is to go down the tunnel behind you and earn us good boy points with the mistress, then we take your things anyway. Pleasing her earns us a nice little bonus."

"Praise the mistress," cackled Alvaro, waving his hands in the air mockingly.

"This mistress you speak of...who is she?" asked Erde.

"You will see very soon," warned Eburhard. "She will be eager to meet you."

"Meet him and eat him!" exclaimed Alvaro, slapping his knee. "She's going to be very pleased with us this time. You're just more fleshy than the others. What a meal you'll make, oh yes."

"You're a lowly worm, Alvaro," grunted Erde.

"The big spooky skeleton got you good, right? It always gets 'em good," sneered Alvaro. "I bet you thought you were the king of the Outer World dealing with those weaklings in the robes. A child could take those boney bastards out."

"I will get out of here and I will kill you both, I assure you," advised Erde, reaching into his pack for bandages.

"I don't think that's very likely now," said Alvaro. "Take a moment and think about your situation. If you can get out of there in one piece, I'll throw myself right off the mountainside for you. Fair?"

"How about you throw yourself from the roof of the cathedral? That way I can watch the earth pulverise your corpse. That would be rather satisfying."

Alvaro spat into the pit. "Make your jokes because you won't get to for much longer. I make my living going to hellscapes like this. Altburg? We've seen it up close. Autun? Been there too.

Helped finish off an Outer Sentinel, I did. I cannot be killed so easily, do you understand?"

"You think that the murder of a demon hunter, sworn to protect our realm is a claim to fame? You're nothing. You are less than any demon or undead in this place."

Alvaro's face was contorted with rage. "You can call me whatever names you want, mate. It doesn't change the fact that an idiot like you fell for our trick and now sits at the bottom of a pit. Face it, Erde of Olfen, you lost."

Erde winced as he pulled the bandage tight and readjusted his armour. "I will see the pair of you soon. Expect me to come straight through those doors carrying your mistress's head. It will be the last thing you see before I cut each of your throats."

The two villains looked at each other and laughed heartily. The pair walked away from the pit, still cackling, and left Erde alone. He could hear Alvaro singing a mocking song that echoed throughout the catacombs.

Erde fully intended to make good on his promise to the devious duo. He slowly climbed to his feet and looked for the tunnel Eburhard spoke of. There it was, an opening in the stone wall that led to more darkness. An unwelcoming sight, but a small glimmer of hope.

The mercenary retreated into the tunnel, clutching his shoulder with one hand and holding his torch with the other. He kept walking until the sounds of merriment faded.

Chapter 4

The Spider Pit

The tunnels beneath the catacombs were dark, damp and dreary. The only sound was the occasional drip of water hitting the stone or the scuttling of an insect somewhere nearby. It was cold but stuffy. Erde wondered if the stuffiness was the tight space itself or his distaste for tight spaces.

He walked through the maze still clutching the hole in his shoulder. Alvaro's bolt had pieced him clean. It was painful, but he could still use his arm. Erde wasn't sure whether that was intentional or not but chose to believe it was. The last thing he wanted to do was underestimate the dastardly pair for whenever he next paid them a visit.

A shadow suddenly moved along the wall ahead. Erde froze and drew his sword. He waited, but it did not reappear. Not naïve enough to believe it a mere trick of the light, the mercenary cautiously continued to walk. A servant of this 'mistress,' perhaps?

There it was again. Erde had a clearer view this time. It was the size of a small shield and dashed along on its many legs. Its back was glossy, yet hairy, and two tiny fangs sat at the front of its head

"Damn spiderlings," spat Erde, familiar with these unnaturally large arachnids. He did not fear them, for they were weaker than the ghouls in a one on one fight, but the last thing he wanted was an enemy creeping up on him in the cover of darkness and spewing toxic venom like rain.

Erde proceeded down the path which eventually opened into a much larger cavern. Small beams of faint moonlight spread out from tiny holes in the ceiling accompanied by the fog. It revealed a dark lake over the edge of a tall ledge. At the edge of the lake, sat five or six dozen of the spiderlings. They were vibrating erratically, then taking it in turns leaping into the air before landing on their original spots. Perhaps they were engaging in a ritual of some sort?

One of the spiderlings crawled around the room and ascended the slope leading towards Erde. It stopped before him and hissed, clicking its two small fangs together. Was it trying to communicate?

"I do not understand," said Erde, cocking his head to the side. "I am not of your race and do not know which tongue you speak with. Let me pass and you shall have no trouble with me." The spiderling let out a small screech and then more of them began to approach.

Erde immediately skewered the spiderling in front of him with his sword. He was not taking any chances, nor would he let himself get outnumbered by the little beasts. The spiderlings rushed to the aid of their fallen brethren, angered by Erde's attack.

Knowing of their fear of fire, Erde swung his torch in an arc and ordered the spiderlings to stay back. "I gave your kin fair warning. Come any closer and you will meet the same fate."

They kept coming, unwilling to back down. With no choice left, Erde began to stab at them. He dispatched seven or eight of the foul arachnids before they retreated. They gave him a wide berth, then leaned back on their spindly legs and lurched forward, spitting their venom.

Erde leapt from the ledge into the water, praying it was not shallow. He plunged deep below and hurriedly swam back to the surface. His soaked torch was useless to him now and he discarded it, not wanting to be slowed down.

He climbed out of the water and began to run down the tunnel near where the spiderlings had been dancing. Hoping there was a way out from here, Erde hurried as fast as he could. He bashed into the corners and scraped his arms on jagged protrusions, but he did not slow down.

Erde emerged into a large cavern and suddenly stopped as a creature descended from the ceiling. Much to his surprise, it was a woman and she stared at him intensely. She had long black hair and pale white skin, wearing a delighted smile. She was quite beautiful...at first. From the waist down, her body turned black and hairy, with eight long legs emerging from her thorax. At the end of each leg was a hand-like protrusion.

"You must be the mistress," said Erde, raising his sword.

The mistress looked ravenous. She crept slowly forward, licking two long fangs. Erde was ready to strike, no matter where she attacked from. The sooner the better, as the spiderlings could not be far behind him.

The mistress spat a web from her mouth and Erde turned to the side, narrowly avoiding the attack. He sprinted forward and stabbed at the mistress, who nimbly leapt over him. She towered over Erde on her long spider legs and swiftly crouched to take a bite from his neck.

Erde dropped to the ground and slashed at one of her legs, cutting it clean off. The mistress emitted a cavern-shaking scream as green blood spilt over the floor. Erde ran out of the way and steadied himself as she used her remaining front leg to try and pull him in.

"You..." uttered the mistress in a cold voice.

Seeing her more closely, Erde spied a large scar on her pale neck. "I will have your head and your men upstairs will see it the moment before I take theirs."

The mistress began to spit venom wildly, bombarding Erde with hundreds of droplets. He turned around and crouched, hoping his armour would take the brunt of it. He felt the back of his neck and arms burning, but he endured.

Erde ran towards the mistress, who reared up, ready to grab the mercenary with her feet and tear him apart. As she made her move, Erde dived underneath her. He rolled and slashed outward, cutting off two more of her legs. The mistress

collapsed and dropped on top of Erde. His sword and legs were pinned underneath her.

Erde suddenly heard a familiar scuttling as the spiderlings burst into the room, coming to aid their mother. He could feel the mistress's blood seeping through his already-drenched clothing.

The half-spider turned to face him; her face filled with fury. As she tilted her head back ready to spit more acid, Erde pulled his knife from his waistband and stabbed her in the abdomen. She yelled and spluttered, her acid spilling down her front and burning her human neck, breasts and arms.

"Yield!" barked Erde, retrieving his knife and ready to stab her again.

"I yield," cried the mistress, tears of pain filling her eyes.

"Banish your children," ordered Erde as the mistress stared at him. "Do it now."

She waved her hand and dismissed the spiderlings, sending them back into the tunnels, then climbed onto her remaining five legs. Erde arose, picking up his sword.

He was dismayed to see that between the acid and the full weight of the spider woman, the blade had shattered. It was barely longer than his dagger, but still sharp enough to deal with her. He remained vigilant in case she made a sudden attack.

"What...do you...want?" sobbed the mistress.

Erde locked eyes with the distraught monster. "I want to return to the surface. I am happy to leave you with your head, should you wish to keep it. It would be a chore for me to carry it around and will only slow me down when I deal with your two minions."

"The worm...the bounty hunter...it is their fault you are here?"

"Yes."

"You can leave, powerful warrior...but you must kill them both. I demand this...as an act of penance," ordered the mistress, suddenly looking equally upset and vengeful as she held her wounds.

Erde stared at her. "What is your name?"

"I am Sabrae...the Spider Queen. Wife of Scaron, God of Spiders. A more powerful enemy...you could not have made."

"Mistress Sabrae. I am a powerful warrior, it is true, but I will need a new weapon to fulfil this task. You have broken my sword, and I am sure that a wife of Scaron would have access to powerful magic and implements."

Sabrae contemplated this for a moment, torn between her hatred of Erde and a desire for vengeance. "Very well...hand me your shattered sword."

"I will give you my sword, but know that my knife remains with me and it is what I will kill you with should you try anything underhanded."

The Spider Queen stared into Erde's eyes, not blinking. She reached out one of her human hands. Erde gathered the broken pieces of his blade and approached her. He passed the Spider Queen the sword and its shards, hoping he would not regret this.

Sabrae laid Erde's sword on the floor and lifted one of her own dismembered legs. The hand at the end of the leg flailed limply as she tossed it on the ground beside the broken sword. She spat her venom onto the floor, creating a ritual circle. She then placed rocks around the circle and stood back.

Erde watched intently as Sabrae began to chant. She spoke in a hissing language, completely foreign to his ears. The acid began to glow a fluorescent green, lighting the whole cavern. Having witnessed many a ritual, the mercenary stood patiently for hours as Sabrae performed her incantation of chaos magic. Interrupting a magical process such as this would be most unwise.

The sword and dismembered leg vibrated violently, and they were enveloped in the same green glow as the circle. The leg shot towards the sword and they were joined together in the light. As the green began to dissipate and the vibrating stopped, Sabrae's chanting slowed and her voice lowered to a whisper before fading to silence.

She gestured to Erde, signalling that he could retrieve his newly imbued blade. He picked it up and examined it. The once-basic longsword was now a darker steel with a purple tint. The cross-guard, handle and pommel had turned black and become segmented, taking on the traits of the Spider Queen's leg.

"It looks pretty and shiny," said Erde, twirling the blade effortlessly, "but what does it do?"

Sabrae stared proudly at her work. "This sword is infused...with my venom. If this sword touches flesh...it will be burned...then numbed. A disabling killer. What you can use...for the two upstairs."

"A horrible fate, but one they deserve," muttered Erde as sheathed the sword. It still fit perfectly into his scabbard.

The Spider Queen stumbled over to Erde and gently caressed his cheek, smiling softly. "I will not forget how you mutilated me...and killed my children. One day...my husband will seek his revenge. This place...was to be my safe haven."

"Scaron had better bring an army if he wants revenge," scoffed Erde, as he batted her hand away. "There is no safe haven for you should there be any retaliation. Consider this a final warning."

"Your attitude...will do you no favours...Xantem will have your corpse. He will place your skull...in the throne at the base of his tree."

"Xantem is one of your minions? Tell him I'll be waiting."

"No," smirked the Spider Queen. "Xantem is the king of this domain. The master...of the dead."

Erde smirked back. "Then I shall have *his* head instead of yours."

"Your overconfidence...will be your undoing. Perhaps, you will learn...humility. The Necropolis has a way of humbling all before death."

"I have come here with a task and I shall see it through to the end. Not even death will stop me, I assure you, Spider Queen."

"What is...your task?"

"I have three companions to find. Their names are Heidi, Waren and Fueur. If you have seen them, you will tell me."

"I have not seen them. Perhaps, I have eaten them...without knowing their names. I do not like to play with my food."

"Should I cut open your stomach and check?" asked Erde, fully intending to follow through on his threat. "I'll stitch it up afterwards so that it matches the scar on your throat."

Sabrae's face bore a look of anger far greater than any Erde had seen so far. "What sort of wretched man...would betray a truce?"

"Truce? You yielded at my command. I owe you nothing."

"I grow tired of you. Leave and do not return. I only demand...the penance."

"I will kill one of them and send the other to you as proof. I make no promises as to which, but one of them will wander through your domain before long," said Erde. "Now guide me back to the surface."

"I was promised a place...to wait out the end of the Era. Instead, I meet...you." She looked downcast as she said this.

"Whether the Era is ending today or five centuries from now is of little consequence to me. Tell me where to go and you will never see me again."

Sabrae's beautiful face broke into a horrible frown as she pointed towards one of the tunnels at the back of her cavern. She then turned her back on Erde and limped weakly down another tunnel, sealing it with a thick web and hiding her from view.

Walking down the tunnel the Spider Queen had pointed to, Erde couldn't help but wonder if it would lead to his death. Those fears were short-lived, however, as the tunnel opened into a large chasm with a spiral staircase circling its way to the top.

The chasm was pitch black and the descent could have led straight to the Inner World. There was no end in sight. Erde ignored it, glad it wasn't another cramped tunnel and walked up the narrow staircase, happy to be going upwards. The early morning light pouring in from overhead gave him a small sense of hope in this bleak city of nightmares.

A figure stood in an alcove across the chasm as Erde ascended. He was a tall man wearing ash-grey metal armour, concealing his entire body. He watched Erde walking up the stairs. The mercenary would not have noticed the observant stranger, had it not been for the embers.

Glowing orange emanated from behind the grill of his helmet and each of the joints, emitting small streams of smoke. He held a greatsword, almost as long as his body, with the tip pointed into the ground. The top half of the blade was molten-hot and more smoke flowed gently upwards from it.

Erde stared at him, but the knight did not move. The mercenary continued climbing towards the surface, exhausted from his many battles, his injuries and his lack of sleep. He had no time to stop and had no desire to antagonise this faceless man.

Reaching the surface, he glanced back towards the alcove, but the knight had disappeared. Erde knew that this was not the last he had seen of him. Whoever this mysterious stalker was, the mercenary knew that he was not as friendly as the Man with Four Faces seemed to be.

Surveying his surroundings, he could once more see the thick wall of fog. Any hopes of finding a secret passage out of Furcht had been dashed. No matter, for he still had companions to find.

Erde walked away from Sabrae's domain and across the rough grass. He looked towards the obscured ball of light in the sky. He was on the outskirts of the city, but at the opposite side from where the entrance lay. Now, he resolved to journey back to the cathedral where the amulet awaited him, draped around the neck of a soon-to-be-dead man.

Chapter 5

Love and Lust

Erde walked along the path cautiously, wary of what may emerge from the fog nearby. His newly enchanted sword, which he affectionately named Sabrae's Leg, was ready to be tested on whatever foe he happened upon first. The blade glistened in the morning light, even with the dense fog refusing to let the sun's rays through.

He was tired, but he did not stop. If he sat down for a moment, he feared he would drift off into sleep. He longed to rest, even for half an hour of uninterrupted sleep, but he could not let himself cave to the temptation. He thought it would have been rather foolish to leave himself so vulnerable in a place so hostile.

The mercenary felt truly alone. When he was on

the road with his companions, they would take watch in shifts. He usually took the first watch, happy to let the others rest. Even thinking about the idea of others sleeping made him want to lay down out of view.

No, he must push on. He had one companion to save and three more to find. The detour that Alvaro and Eburhard had sent him on had wasted far more time than he was comfortable with. Once they were dead and Troyes was saved, he would take a few hours of rest.

Erde's ears pricked up as the sound of very faint whispers reached him. They were close, but he could not make out what they said. Erde strained his eyes, trying to see through the fog as he listened for the origin.

"Come to us," whispered a woman seductively.

"This way," whispered another.

Erde did not answer them, sensing a malevolent trick. He would find them and kill them, preventing them from harming anybody else unfortunate enough to happen upon this place. Who would be so stupid as to follow them? The mercenary thought this as he wandered in their direction.

"Follow me," whispered yet another woman, her voice warming Erde's heart. It was familiar, yet strange. A bizarre sensation.

The whispers continued to beckon him forward, luring him to wherever they lay in wait. Keeping a watchful eye on his barely visible surroundings, he grew closer to the voices.

He approached a small set of steps that led to a temple crafted from fine white stone. The building was round and barely larger than a house. It was far from the majesty of the cathedral, but a pleasant sight in this otherwise deserted region of the city.

"Come inside," whispered the first woman's voice.

Erde pushed one of the doors open and walked in. Adjusting his eyes to the lack of fog, he took in the unexpected spectacle.

He was in a circular room with a large marble statue of a naked woman atop a pedestal. She had a perfectly symmetrical face, finely carved in exquisite detail. Her hair was braided and hung over her left shoulder, covering one of her breasts. Little about her slender figure was left to the imagination. In her right hand, she held a harp and her left hand was stretched overhead.

Beds adorned the outside of the room, all covered in soft white sheets and pillows. On the bed were naked women and men, all silently engaging in amorous acts that would astound even the most prolific women of the night. Erde averted his eyes, preferring not to watch.

An unoccupied woman with dark brown hair approached Erde. She was the only clothed woman in the room, but it barely made a difference. She wore a white gown that was nearly transparent, clearly revealing her whole body.

Her green eyes sparkled as she whispered to him, running her fingers up his arm. "I am without a mate. Will you indulge me?"

"No," said Erde, staring her straight in the eye. He wanted to make a move for his dagger but could not bring himself to do so. The touch of a woman after so long was something he longed for, yet he could not long for this woman. He fought the urge.

"Why not? Does my appearance displease you?" she asked.

"I have a wife and I would die before betraying her. No woman, demon of lust or otherwise, will break me. I suggest you do not try lest it be the end of you."

Erde ignored her continued attempts at pulling him in closer and walked towards a small door at the left of the room. He wanted to leave, but he had to make sure that Waren and Fueur had not fallen for the tricks of the whisperers.

It dawned on him that he did not truly want to follow the whispers. Why did he do it? Was he already under their evil spell? Was it a matter of time before he broke? He must finish his search and leave this place at once.

The door led to a garden, enclosed by a stone wall. Curiously, there was no fog in sight. Neatly trimmed purple and red flowers were dotted about the clearing and a tree sat at the centre, bearing perfect yellow pears. They looked ripe and juicy, but Erde did not trust that they weren't yet another trap.

Much like inside, there were at least a dozen pairs of naked people giving into their lust. Not one of them seemed to notice Erde's presence. He was confident that none of these men was the gaunt Waren or the tall, fair Fueur.

An unaccompanied female with silky blonde hair, wearing a loose white gown emerged from behind the tree and approached Erde. Her face was all too familiar.

"I am in need of a man to satisfy me. Would you care to join me?" she whispered, running her fingers over his neck.

"Heidi?" Erde was aghast. "What have they done to you?"

Heidi looked confused and softly touched Erde's cheek. "I do not know this name. Will you come closer?"

Erde pushed her away as she leaned in to kiss him. "You have fallen afoul of their magic. We are leaving immediately."

"We must be together in V'andrya's temple.".

"Heidi, it is me. It is Erde. You must remember me. Troyes? Waren? Fueur?" asked Erde desperately, staring into her light blue eyes. Eyes that he had longed to see for so long. "What about Josef and Marta?"

Heidi lowered her robe and wrapped herself around Erde, but he pushed her off. He grabbed the robe and covered her naked body. Pulling her by the forearm, he led her towards the door.

Suddenly, all of the men and women stopped their intercourse. They all looked very angry, their faces contorting in inhuman ways. Their true forms were revealed, but Heidi remained unchanged.

As Erde dragged her to the door, she continued whispering seductive phrases. He ignored them and as he reached for the door he was bitten by one of the fornicators.

Erde released Heidi and punched the whisperer in the eye socket. It recoiled in pain while the mercenary drew his sword.

The whisperers all charged towards him, even Heidi's face was now twisted into a demonic visage. Erde could not look at her and tossed her aside. He slashed wildly at the lust demons, the acid from Sabrae's Leg burning their skin before they dropped to the ground, numbed by the venom. They were not strong, much like the ghouls and spiderlings, but they were numerous.

They bit and scratched Erde, but he killed them one by one. Each time Heidi attacked, he threw her to the floor. He could not bear to kill her.

The fight raged across the garden, the limp whisperers dragging themselves across the ground like zombies. The flowers were torn to shreds, the grass trampled into the dirt. At the end of the fight, the ground was soaked red with blood.

Erde stood there, his sword in his hand, holding Heidi back by the throat. She hissed and screamed, trying to claw at him. "You have desecrated the temple! You must pay!" she yelled. Her face was vengeful and murder was all that was left in her eyes.

"I'm sorry," muttered Erde, fighting back tears. "I will avenge you...I promise. I will tell Josef and Marta that you love them."

Erde released Heidi and swung his sword in a wide arc as she leapt towards him, beheading her with one swift cleave.

The mercenary fell to his knees, breathing rapidly. He prayed to the True One and begged that Heidi's soul could escape this realm and be guided to the Inner World. He prayed that one day he would see her again. He prayed that Waren and Fueur were still alive, not afflicted with a similar fate. A fate that was far worse than death.

Erde arose and walked to the courtyard door. He knew what lay inside waiting for him and he was ready to face them. He threw open the door to face the other demons that had ceased their fornication.

All of the men and women were approaching, ready to tear the flesh from his bones, even the brunette in the robe. Erde slashed at the demons, cutting three of the whisperers' torsos and spilling their guts across the floor. They yelled with blood-curdling screams as their flesh burned from the toxins.

"You will all die today," roared Erde. He furiously impaled, dismembered and beheaded the approaching demons. Just as the possessed Heidi had been vengeful and murderous, so was he.

He was scratched and bitten, but his anger was too great. With renewed strength, he slaughtered everyone in the temple. He was cut, he was bruised, and the hole in his shoulder ached, but he did not care. They had to pay.

As the demons lay dead on the floor, the beaten and bloody Erde walked over to the beds. He hacked at the wooden frames and piled the planks around the statue. He would not allow an inch of this place to remain standing.

He spat on the statue before pouring the little oil he had remaining from his pack over the wood. Erde had not slept enough to replenish his magic, but he forced himself to emit a single spark. It may have been luck, it may have been anger, but he willed the spell from his fingertips. It ignited the oil and, before long, a raging fire was burning.

Erde took his leave and departed from the burning, massacred temple. He did not look back, walking into the fog as the smell of smoke filled his nostrils. He found the road to the main city and kept his eye out for any landmarks that would lead him to the cathedral.

"Our paths cross again," came a voice from the

fog. The Man with Four Faces emerged from nowhere. "I see that you've taken quite the beating since our last meeting. Is that a new hole in your shoulder or was that always there?"

"Are you following me?" asked Erde.

"Perhaps I am. Perhaps it is you following me? We may never know," pondered the mysterious wanderer, giving a nonchalant shrug.

"I would love nothing more than to indulge your riddles, but I have pressing business."

The Man with Four Faces approached tepidly. "May I?" he asked, gesturing towards Erde's shoulder.

Erde did not answer, but the man approached anyway. He raised his hands and a soft glow emitted from them. Erde felt a sharp twinge as the hole in his shoulder was mended. It was as good as new.

"Thank you," he said.

The man's helmet bore its happy face. "Is that pillar of smoke your doing? What a show you've provided for me today, very exciting. The shrine of V'andrya, if I'm not mistaken."

"Yes," replied Erde. "There was no place more deserving of being reduced to ash than that wretched hole."

"You're alone," said the man, his face turning to a sad face. "Does this mean what I think it means? Your companion...she was there."

Erde lowered his head, unsure of what to say. He nodded silently.

"I am sorry for your loss. Truly."

The two stood on the road quietly for a while. It was not an uncomfortable silence, but the man knew Erde would not be placated by mere words.

"I should take my leave," said Erde, breaking the silence.

"Do you not want a question answered? Perhaps something about your oth—"

"Who is Xantem?"

The man's helmet rotated to neutral. "You know this name already? It took me months of being here to learn of him. Amusingly, it was him that I sought without realising it. The Elixir of Life, they said. What a fool I was."

Erde simply stared at the Man with Four Faces.

The man took the hint. "Yes, to the point. Xantem is a lich, an undead of great power. He combines the divine power of the Inner World deity, Mallabeth, with the corruptive force of demonic sorcery. The ghouls up ahead? They are his handiwork. Even if you cut them into a thousand pieces, he will reassemble them eventually. Burning them to ashes is one of the only effective disposal methods I have found.

"The Pig Warden is one of his twisted undead creations too. There are hundreds of weird experiments throughout the city, some I'm sure that even I have yet to see. Which is saying something as I have seen more than I like. The evil roots of this place go deep, I'm afraid. I mean that in the most literal sense."

"He created this place? This false Furcht, or whatever it is? The Necropolis?" asked Erde.

The man stopped to think for a moment. "I will permit that follow-on question as I deem it relevant. No, he did not, but his ancestors did. I am not as well versed in the history of this place as some. If you want to know more, seek out Leer in the library."

"Leer?" asked Erde.

"I will answer no more questions, but I do recommend speaking with Leer if you seek more answers. You can find the library by finding the harpies."

"Why are you playing this game? One question and one answer. What is the point?"

"That's all I have to say for now," said the man, turning away. He looked back briefly. "Once again, my condolences. It is never easy to lose those that we care about. Good luck, stranger."

"You have never asked my name," said Erde.

"Nor you mine. Do you really think my name is the Man with Four Faces? It would have been very unfortunate for me had my parents named me after a helmet I did not own when my mother birthed me," replied the man, disappearing into the fog.

Erde stood alone at the edge of the city. He knew it would be pointless to ask more of the man. He was as enigmatic as he was irritating. Perhaps he wasn't always this way and the city had maddened him, yet he did not seem to be insane.

The mercenary decided it was not worth pondering this again and wandered forwards on the road straight ahead, in search of the city streets. The occasional ghoul came across his path, perhaps tired of the same streets, and was beheaded with ease.

The stony road was short, but Erde tread carefully. His exhaustion had caught up with him once more and he felt as though he could collapse. The only thing that kept him going was a small lingering glimmer of hope.

Jordan Allen

Chapter 6

Vengeance

The Cathedral of the True One, in all its glory, loomed above Erde. His face was sunken, his body battered and bruised, while his soul weighed heavily upon him. He had never felt less worthy of entering such a place.

He pushed the door open, knowing Alvaro would be waiting on a balcony above. He must be quick to catch the worm by surprise. There could be no room for error this time.

Erde pushed the heavy doors open and ran inside. He sought cover behind a pillar and waited. He heard no sound from Alvaro's hiding spot. Perhaps he was not here.

Erde reached into his pack and grabbed the empty bottle that had once contained his oil. He lobbed it in front of the doors and it was immediately struck by a bolt, smashing into a thousand pieces.

"You're a slippery one, I'll give you that," chuckled Alvaro. "I was hoping it would be more fresh meat for the mistress and we would be getting our nice little bonus."

"You will be getting no more bonuses from her, I'm afraid," called Erde. "Long black hair, half of her body is a spider. That sounds like her, right? Her head is in my pack. It'll be yours next."

Alvaro scoffed dismissively. "I ain't afraid of you. In case you hadn't noticed, you don't have anywhere to run and you won't reach me. You can walk out those doors and never return. I'll give you a chance, just this once."

Erde did not believe the deceitful cretin. He threw his knife at the doors and sprinted in the opposite direction. Alvaro took the bait and shot at the blade firmly wedged in the wooden planks.

The thief reloaded his crossbow as quickly as he could, but Erde had already crossed the room and reached the back staircase by the time Alvaro was ready.

Erde could not wait at the spiral staircase long in case Alvaro had other dirty tricks up his sleeve. The mercenary had images flashing in his mind of a bottle of acid smashing him across the head or a firebomb burning his flesh. He wiped the images from his mind and bounded up the stairs.

"You should just give up, mate," called Alvaro. "I know you're behind that wall. The second you come out, you're dead. I won't fall for your tricks a second time."

"Are you sure?" asked Erde. "You're as thick as

the ghouls, you little worm. You're as ugly as them too, that's for sure. Are you too scared to face me one on one?"

"Scared?" scoffed Alvaro, his voice shaking. "I ain't scared of no one. You think I'll come over there and give you the advantage? Afraid not."

Erde began to cluck. It was silly and didn't sound very much like a chicken, but the more he could anger the thief the better. He clucked louder and louder trying to throw Alvaro off.

The thief was enraged. "There's going to be nothing left of you when I'm done. You hear? Death by the mistress was a kindness."

Erde took off both of his boots and his pack, clucking louder still. He threw one of his boots, then the other, then his pack. Alvaro ignored the boots but took the final bait and shot the pack as it flew through the air.

Once Erde heard the click of the crossbow and the whoosh of the bolt, he ran. Alvaro had a look of sheer terror in his eyes as Erde slashed at the crossbow, cutting it in two. The thief fell backwards and Erde planted a foot on his throat.

"Please...I was only d-d-doing what I was t-t-told," stammered the snivelling worm. "Don't k-k-kill me."

"Kill you?" asked Erde, cocking his head to the side. "No, no. I have a much better idea. I'm not going to kill you, but I'm going to need you to place your hand on the floor. This won't hurt...for long."

Alvaro pleaded and begged, but Erde shook his head. Sniffling, Alvaro placed his hand on the floor. It was trembling. Erde jammed his sword at the thief's hand and chopped off Alvaro's index and middle fingers.

"Aaaaargh!" cried Alvaro.

"Do you see this beautiful sword?" asked Erde as he wiped the blood on Alvaro's armour. "It was made from the leg of your mistress, Sabrae. The acid will burn for a moment and then it should numb quickly. I hope it doesn't make firing your crossbow too difficult for you. That would be an awful shame."

"What...what do you want?" asked Alvaro, his voice still trembling.

"I want you to take me to Eburhard. You've received your punishment, but he has not. I'm afraid he will be less lucky than you. If you do that for me, I won't kill you."

"Yes...yes, of course."

Erde patted Alvaro down, checking for any hidden weapons. Once he was satisfied, he retrieved the rope from his pack to bind the whimpering man's hands. He then dragged him down the stairs and through the doors to the catacombs, but not before retrieving his boots and knife.

"Will he know we're coming?" asked Erde.

Alvaro quickly shook his head. "No. He only gets on the ground when he hears the last of the bones rattling on the floor."

The skeletons had been reset from Erde's previous visit and he handily dealt with each of them as he passed, pulling Alvaro behind him. They reached the barred window and Erde spotted the familiar giant skeleton. A loathsome deception.

"Where did you find that?" Erde asked. "It's convincing."

"It's real," said Alvaro. "Eburhard knows some of them divine spells that freeze skeletons. It's why he's the one who waits down 'ere."

Erde navigated the last few corridors and walked into the large room, dragging Alvaro along. He walked over to the window with the bars and tied Alvaro's rope to it.

Eburhard was still on the floor, he must not have realised who was paying him a visit. As Erde approached, Eburhard continued to keep still. Erde raised his blade and prepared to strike at the gap between the man's helmet and neck.

Erde was suddenly flung backwards by a powerful push. When Erde looked up, he saw Eburhard on his feet, one hand raised and the other clutching his own sword.

"You are a fool to have returned," said Eburhard. "It will be your last mistake."

Erde grunted as he climbed to his feet.

"Come cut me loose!" called Alvaro, tugging on the rope..

"How did he get past you?" asked Eburhard. "You were meant to be keeping a close eye on the door."

"He's a sneaky one with a few trick of his own. Don't underestimate him.

Eburhard kept his hand raised, ready to use the Push spell should Erde come close. Erde ran to the side, using the giant skeleton for cover. Eburhard circled around, trying to position Erde in front of the pit.

The mercenary thumped his sword into the skeleton's foot, sending it crashing down. Both men ran from the falling bones as they hit the floor.

Eburhard tripped and Erde pounced on him, slicing his throat with his knife. The armoured man was trying to breathe, unable to vocalise any words. He could not scream and he could not beg for help, but he grasped his sword tightly.

Erde dragged him by the legs and rolled him into the pit. He walked over to Alvaro, who watched in terror, and untied his hands.

"I'm free to go then?" asked Alvaro, a look of relief creeping over his face.

"Yes," said Erde, placing the tip of his sword at the back of Alvaro's neck.

"What is this?" demanded Alvaro. "I did what you asked, didn't I?"

"You're free to go, but you must leave through the pit."

"You're having a laugh, right?"

"No. The mistress is expecting you."

Alvaro's eyes widened in horror. "She ain't dead...you cut a deal with her?"

"You can discuss it with her yourself, if she gives you that chance. She's not best pleased that you sent me down there."

Alvaro clasped his hands together. "Please, mate. Don't do this. You'll never have to see me again."

"Walk," ordered Erde, pressing the sword into the worm's neck.

Alvaro complied and walked to the edge of the pit. He gave Erde a pleading look, but the mercenary shook his head. Erde grabbed the amulet from around the worm's neck and kicked him square in the back. He tumbled in, landing a few feet from Eburhard. The armoured man was still struggling to breathe as blood gushed from his throat.

"You're a bastard!" screamed Alvaro. "A dirty, rotten piece of scum. I'll get outta here and see that you pay. Mark my words."

"Don't keep her waiting," said Erde as he turned his back on the pit and walked away.

*

Erde exited the cathedral and was immediately blinded by the sunlight. It felt as though years had passed since he last laid eyes on that beautiful glowing orb in the sky, but it was only yesterday morning. The amulet was working and he was ready to take his chances with the ghouls and the Pig Warden.

He walked down the steps and onto the streets, still ensuring that he was cautious, but no longer feeling the paranoia he had experienced only hours ago. He did not want to let his guard down, but he found it hard to suppress his relief.

The ghouls covered the town and each street or alleyway Erde passed seemed to house more of them. They were everywhere, but how poor their sight and hearing were became obvious. Erde understood how The Man with Four Faces had grown so confident in a world like this.

The mercenary roamed the town, trying to familiarise himself more with the layout should he be unfortunate enough to lose his amulet and need to rely on memory. He listened for the loud stomping of the ugly behemoth of a swine, but it was not nearby.

Erde wandered into the town square where the fountain stood, a place familiar to him now. If he could attract it, this was the place to do it. He held his fingers to his lips and blew a piercing whistle that echoed across the square.

"What are you doing?" whispered a voice. A man in full-leather armour crept out from a doorway and looked around rapidly, unable to see Erde through the fog.

"I suggest you get out of here," Erde called. "I'm going to draw as many ghouls in as I can."

"For what purpose? You can't fight them all when you can't see them coming."

"They will fall, I assure you. The ghouls and the big pig."

"You have given into madness already, my friend. I wish you luck, but I will not help you."

"Then run!" barked Erde.

The startled man sprinted clumsily away from the square. Erde did not take the time to consider what the man was doing here. Perhaps he was a bounty hunter, perhaps he was a treasure hunter. If he was too cowardly to help fight the common enemy, he was not worth a second thought.

Ghouls ran towards Erde from the surrounding streets. There was at least half a dozen of them. Erde cut each of them down with ease as he let out loud shouts. He was going to make sure the Pig Warden found him and he was going to take his hand to free Troyes.

Erde killed ghoul after ghoul, impaling some and beheading others. One unfortunate undead lost all four of his limbs and struggled helplessly on the cobblestones. It was almost sad, but whoever's body this once was had long departed from it. No sympathy would be given to these abominations.

A crash echoed from the north, followed by

another and then another. It was him. Erde killed the last of the ghouls that had answered the call and ran inside one of the houses. He climbed to the second floor and waited by the open window for his quarry to appear.

It wasn't long before the Pig Warden emerged into the square, sniffing and snorting. He was as ugly as ever. The towering, hunched abomination of an undead wandered towards the large pile of ghouls. There were at least thirty corpses piled, Erde had lost count after the first dozen.

Erde grabbed a small wooden horse from a shelf nearby and dropped it from the window before pressing himself against the wall. The Pig Warden stomped over and crouched down to look at the horse. It sniffed once more, trying to pick up a scent from the child's toy. This was Erde's chance.

He jumped from the window with his sword held in front of him and skewered the Pig Warden in the back. The beast let out an agonising roar as Erde rolled away, waiting for the monster to fall to the ground, but it did not fall to the ground.

It stood up and turned towards him. It reached around to its back and pulled out Sabrae's Leg, tossing it across the square. There was no chance of Erde outrunning the beast in the wide-open square, he would have to distract him first.

The Pig Warden lowered itself and charged at Erde, who drew his knife. He jumped aside, narrowly avoiding the full weight of the beast. He ran towards it and stabbed it repeatedly in the leg, but it elbowed him forcefully. Erde fell to the ground and rushed to return to his feet as the beast swiped at him.

He jammed his knife into its hand to block the

attack but still took a bad scrape to the arm from its gnarled fingernails. The beast lowered its head to bite him. He quickly freed his knife from its hand and jammed it into the Pig Warden's dripping snout. It roared in pain again and Erde used the distraction to run across the square and retrieve his sword.

As he spun around to face the beast, it was upon him once more. It swung at Erde who parried with Sabrae's Leg, then kicked the Pig Warden in the groin. A normal man would have been brought to the floor by the kick, but the beast was no longer human. It was unfazed by the kick and used its other hand to grab Erde's arm. He lifted him high and slammed him into the ground.

Erde yelled in pain and the Pig Warden leapt on top of him, ready to finish the job. Erde reached up with one of his hands and grabbed the knife in its snout. He pulled it out and stabbed the beast in the eye. It recoiled and stood upright as Erde sprung to his feet, drew his sword back and cleaved the monster's left hand off.

The beast was in shock, so he swung his sword at its other exposed hand. The hand hit the stone with a heavy thud and the monster lunged at Erde, its jaw wide open. Erde thrust the blade inside its mouth. It weakly tried to close its jaw; all energy depleted. The Pig Warden fell to the ground with a crash and Erde removed his sword. It would not be troubling him again anytime soon.

He walked over to each hand and removed all of the fingers, stashing them in his pack. The mercenary, satisfied that the beast was not standing up until his master found him, walked westwards in search of the guardhouse once more.

*

The worm looked up from the pit and could see that there was indeed no way back up. As Eburhard was dying, there was no chance he would be able to heal himself or reattach Alvaro's fingers that lay upstairs in the cathedral. There was not much time left and no easy way back to the surface without him.

"Eburhard," said Alvaro, crawling over to his co-conspirator. "I think it's time that one of us made good on our deal. I would say I'm sorry it's you that pays the price, but I'm sure both of us hoped it would be the other. It's been fun, mate. I'll drink to you whenever I get out of the Necropolis."

Eburhard gave a weak nod while clutching his throat as Alvaro hurriedly removed the dying man's cuirass. Alvaro grabbed Eburhard's sword and raised it high above his head. The thief's hands were trembling, perhaps from anxiety, perhaps from the loss of a couple of digits.

"Do...it..." squeaked Eburhard, straining to speak.

"Wish me luck in the tunnels, mate. I'm going to need some luck this time."

"Good...luck..."

"I'll make it quick."

Alvaro stabbed Eburhard in the chest and haphazardly cut his heart out. He grabbed the bloody organ with his fully-fingered hand and ran into the tunnels, weakly grasping the sword with his mutilated hand. He knew a way out of the

Necropolis, all that stood in his way were the spiders in the darkness ahead.

Chapter 7

A Fountain of Knowledge

As Erde walked down the familiar tunnel underneath the guardhouse, a faint song reached his ears. The singer's voice was deep and powerful, but he would find no work as a bard.

The grey woods of the north
Call all of us forth
Welcoming back those who roam

The red fire glows bright
Throughout the whole night
Reminding us that we are home

As a people, we're one
Our bonds never undone

Even with the change of the tide

Come join me, my friends
When the Outer World ends
We will stay by each other's side

Erde knew the song well, it was written by Fueur one night when the group were lost in a forest, in search of a bandit. Fueur did not sing it again after, but Troyes and Erde kept it alive. It now seemed more important than ever to remember it.

Erde approached with one of the Pig Warden's fingers in hand. "It's a wonder that the metal hasn't curled from your less-than-dulcet tones. It would have meant much less effort on my part, friend."

Troyes let out a guttural laugh. "I was starting to wonder if you were dead."

"I am not easily killed," replied Erde as he tried one of the Pig Warden's distorted fingernails on the lock. It clicked immediately and he swung the door open, freeing Troyes at last. "You should know that by now."

The outlander climbed to his feet and walked out of the dingy cell as Erde dumped the rest of the Pig Warden's fingers on the floor. "Thank you, Erde. It's good to see your leg truly has healed, but I can't help noticing the your latest bruises and scratches."

"It's nothing. I will tend to them properly when we get out of here. My worst injury has already been mended."

Troyes stood beside Erde. "I owe you more than you could possibly imagine." While Erde was a tall man, Troyes stood taller still. He towered over everybody he met.

"I'm glad I could free you, but I...I have bad news, Troyes."

Troyes's face fell. "Who?"

"Heidi. The lust demons of V'andrya claimed her and I was forced to kill her."

Troyes closed his eyes for a moment. When he reopened them, he had a look of resolve on his face. "We will avenge her by razing this entire accursed city. I promise you that."

Erde nodded. "Do you know where we might find Waren and Fueur? I understand it has been some time..."

Troyes shook his head. "I do not know where they are. I never laid eyes on Fueur in this place and Waren...well, you know how he is. He immediately talked about how he must uncover the mysteries of Furcht. I do not think he was concerned when we were separated in the fog."

"If he is seeking to uncover the mysteries of Furcht, then perhaps he ventured to the library? The Man with Four Faces advised me that if we wanted to know more about the Necropolis, then we should seek out Leer in the library. It stands to reason that if Waren knows of this library, that's where he may be."

"Who is this man and why does he have four faces?" asked Troyes, visibly confused.

"A mysterious stranger that has given me reliable advice during my time here. I would hesitate to call him a friend, but he is certainly not an enemy. We should take what help we can get right now."

"Your judgement is sound, so I trust that he is indeed reliable. You know the way to this library?"

asked Troyes.

"I was told to find the harpies."

"Ah," said Troyes, scratching his large, stubbly chin, "then we are in luck. I tried to climb the mountain when I arrived, thinking that it may be free of the fog and I could learn the layout of the city. I was accosted by skeletal harpies and had to retreat. Two of us should make it easier."

Erde removed the amulet and held it out to Troyes. "Lead the way. You should be able to see the fog without this."

Troyes pushed the amulet back. "No. I know where to go. Keep that in case we get separated again. I will be fine."

Erde placed the amulet back around his neck and led Troyes through the tunnels, up the stone staircase and through the cellar door. Stepping into the derelict city again, Erde felt the weight of his tiredness. He said nothing and followed Troyes through the winding streets.

They tore through a dozen houses, seeking a weapon for Troyes to use. The best they could find was a rusty sword, but Troyes did not mind. "If it's sharp enough to stab, I can use it well," he said.

The occasional lurking ghoul attacked, but Erde and Troyes had no trouble separating their heads from their bodies. Troyes chuckled as the duo walked through the town square and he saw the handless remains of the Pig Warden. He stopped to give the brute a good kick before continuing northwards towards the mountain path.

The path ahead split in two, the first leading towards the passageway into this twisted, alternate Furcht. The second, the steeper path, was the road less travelled. The cobblestones were covered in thick moss and became sparse a short way up.

The fog did not ease up as the pair climbed. The path weaved in and out of small caves. It would have been treacherous even without the fog and Erde was never more grateful for the amulet.

"Wait," said Erde, spotting something hovering in the distance by the cliffside.

"Do you see them?" asked Troyes, straining to see through the thick cloud. "I know we are close."

Erde nodded as he stared at the skinless, featherless harpies. They were the size of a human woman, but in place of arms, they had wings and talon-like feet. All that was left of these particular harpies were bones, yet they still flapped their bare skeletal wings and stayed aloft. These unfortunate creatures must have been yet another experiment of Xantem.

Erde turned to Troyes. "Stick to the rock wall on your left. If you step too far to the right, they'll drag you off the cliff. Ready?"

Troyes picked up a large rock and signalled that he was ready. Erde charged forward and five harpies whirled around and darted forward. They split into two groups; three attacked Erde and the remaining two attacked Troyes.

Erde swung at the harpies as they dived and clawed at him. He took a number of nasty scratches to the neck before grabbing one of their wings and slamming it into the cliff wall. The other two backed off momentarily before moving into flanking positions. They lunged towards Erde simultaneously, grabbing both of his arms.

Meanwhile, Troyes bashed the large rock he found into the skull of one of the harpies, smashing it into a dozen pieces. The other harpy grabbed him, but Troyes hugged it tightly, breaking its ribs. This was the reason he was usually first into battle when the band were on a job. More intelligent foes usually got the idea and escaped while they could.

The two harpies pulled at Erde's arms, trying to rip them from their sockets, but he dug deep. He clenched hard and jerked his arms together, forcing both harpies to collide in the air above him. They fell to the ground and Erde stamped on one of their skulls while Troyes smashed the other's skull with his rock.

"That counts as three for me," joked Troyes.

"You can tell yourself that, but you will always know I did the hard work," smirked Erde.

Erde had been avoiding thinking about Heidi's death and having Troyes around helped distract him. Troyes had always been simultaneously the most fearsome warrior and light-hearted member of the band. Even when they were bloodied and broken, the two would often make light of dark situations. It irked both Heidi and Fueur to no end, while Waren had never made as much as a pun in his life.

The duo continued along the cliffside path and stumbled upon a cave where the fog began to dissipate. There were more harpies inside, all perched on high rocks or stalagmites. They descended upon the men, who brought them swiftly to the ground in a cascade of bones.

"What's that?" said Troyes, holding up his hand to stop Erde.

Erde listened carefully. If Troyes said he had heard something, he had heard something. The outlander's hearing was as keen as a dog's. It took a few seconds, but Erde heard the clink of metal on the path outside. Both men ran back towards the cave entrance. Erde hoped it was the Man with Four Faces, but feared it was someone else.

As the mouth of the cave opened up, Erde's fears were confirmed. A suit of ash-grey armour approached. It held a greatsword, while a helmet glowed a bright orange from behind the grill. It was the man from the chasm alcove in Sabrae's domain.

"I have seen this man before," said Erde. "Let's retreat to the cave where you'll have a better line of sight."

"No. We do not want to be beset upon by harpies should he want a fight."

The knight stopped walking and swung his greatsword effortlessly. He put one foot in front of the other and held his sword forwards with two hands. He was waiting for Erde and Troyes to make the first move.

Erde and Troyes moved apart, Erde standing to the left by the cliffside while Troyes stayed near the right, where the rock wall was now positioned. Both men raised their swords, Erde with Sabrae's Leg and Troyes with his rusty blade.

The mercenary duo remained steadfast, not wanting to give the ashen knight any advantage. If they moved too close, he would sweep them with his sword before they got near him.

Suddenly, Troyes grabbed a rock from the ground and hurled it at the knight, who blocked it with his ease. Erde charged forward and struck at a small gap in his leg armour. The knight rapidly parried with his blade while Troyes joined the fray.

The knight was fast and fearless. He blocked with his greatsword, each of his arms and each of his legs. Each impact seemed a mere inconvenience to him. Erde locked him in a clinch while Troyes struck at his head. He headbutted Troyes's sword, deflecting the attack.

Erde thrust his sword at the knight's neck and his head bent back with a horrible crack, as though he had broken his spine, but he suddenly jerked his head back into position with a click once Erde withdrew his weapon.

Erde yelled loudly and wrapped his arms around the knight, lifting him above the ground. Erde moved towards the cliff to throw the man into the foggy abyss below. As he approached the edge, the knight broke free and kicked him backwards to the ground.

Troyes roared a battle cry and charged forward, tackling the man over the edge of the cliff. The knight fell from view, leaving Troyes dangling over the edge. Erde had only just managed to grab his friend's ankle with both hands, saving him from falling to his death below.

"I can't...pull you up," grunted Erde, clenching hard and tightening his grip.

"Give me a moment and do not let go," called Troyes. The outlander grabbed onto the rocky protrusions in the cliff face and pushed himself upwards. "Pull!"

Erde pulled as Troyes pushed himself up and over the edge, back onto solid ground. Erde fell back and lay there for a moment, the last of his energy spent.

"Are you...a maniac?" he puffed.

"A practical solution for a desperate situation," said Troyes, cracking a wide grin.

"You were...a dead man."

"Yet here I am. Thank you for saving me, once again."

"You're...welcome."

"Next time, perhaps I will save you from death."

The fearless barbarian stood up and reached out his hand to Erde. He pulled his friend to his feet and the two walked back into the cave, away from the seemingly bottomless drop.

"This fellow, how did you survive him before?" asked Troyes. "He bested us in a two-on-one fight. I've never seen anything like it."

"We were separated by a chasm. This is the first time I've seen him up close. I pray it's the last. If he's another undead, I suspect tumbling off a cliff is not the end of him."

Erde had explained to Troyes on the journey up the mountainside most things that had happened since he arrived in Furcht, but had forgotten all about the brief encounter with the knight until he heard the clank of metal approaching.

The duo trudged through the cave and dealt with a dozen more harpies along the way. Eventually, the cave opened into a larger cavern and the men could see a giant harpy lying in a nest the size of a pond. The harpy stirred as they approached, sitting upright and turning her large head with her empty eye sockets towards them.

"You have killed my children, and you have come to kill me?" asked the skeleton in a squawking voice.

"Your children were already dead, and I'm sure they will rise again," replied Erde. "We have no interest in you, we are seeking the library."

"The library does not have visitors for nearly a year, yet now I have three in the space of a few weeks. Very well, you may enter."

The harpy mother squawked very loudly. Her warbling tone echoed throughout the cavern and an opening appeared in the cave wall. The opening did not lead into darkness, but into a swirling vortex of blue and purple. It was hypnotising to look at.

"Go," squawked the harpy.

"How do you know that we can trust you not to lead us to our deaths?" asked Troyes.

"She is not to be trusted," came a voice from the portal, as a gaunt man with long, white hair emerged, "but she is not lying now. She has been tasked with guarding the entrance to the library in exchange for being allowed to remain here. It is a deal that keeps her bound to the lord of the library."

Waren walked over to his friends and gave them a formal salute. Erde and Troyes returned the salute, pleased to be reunited with another of their companions.

"I suspected that you may be here," said Erde. "What would a mystical library be without a sorcerer to cover its secrets?"

"You look well," said Troyes. "I'm glad to see that you are safe."

"Likewise, my friends," said Waren, before turning towards Erde. "It is not a surprise that you travelled here, but I do wish you had not."

"Troyes said more or less the same thing," replied Erde.

"Come," said Waren, beckoning his friends to the portal, "we have much to discuss."

Erde and Troyes followed Waren to the portal. Waren gestured towards the vortex and Erde stepped in first. He was ripped from the cave and felt as though he was plummeting from the sky, before just-as-suddenly landing on his feet in a lit, but shadowy room.

The light came from the archways in the ceiling at least three hundred feet above. The ceiling itself was intricately patterned, featuring depictions of saints and angels fighting against hordes of demons.

The room was separated into a dozen open floors with bookshelves lining the walls. Wooden staircases and walkways connected the floors in a chaotic, yet beautiful manner. The ground floor, where Erde stood, had more tall bookshelves throughout. There must have been millions of books in this building, more than any mortal could read in a lifetime.

Men in black robes patrolled the room, holding lanterns that emitted a blue glow. One of them approached Erde, who saw what lay underneath their hoods. A large brain with a gaping mouth below it stared at him, or at least it would have done if it had eyes. Three tentacles protruded from its cheeks and floated eerily in the air as though they were underwater. It stopped in front of the mercenary for a moment before turning around and continuing its patrol.

"I do not like this place," muttered Troyes. Erde had not noticed him emerge from the portal, too distracted by the grandiosity of the library and its unsettling inhabitants.

"You do not have to like it," said Waren, as he appeared, "but you must respect it. It is a place filled with knowledge that you cannot comprehend, but more important than anything you can imagine. The demons here will not harm you without cause. Now come with me. I will take you to see my master."

Chapter 8

Unfamiliar Walls

"Your master?" asked Erde, alarmed at what Waren had said.

Waren nodded. "As I said before, we have much to discuss."

"I'm not moving until you tell us what you mean by master," demanded Troyes.

"Is it Leer?" asked Erde.

"Master Leer, the Sage of the Walls, is the master of this place. He has accepted me as his apprentice and is therefore my master."

Troyes looked disheartened. "You do not plan to return with us to our world, do you?"

"No," said Waren, avoiding eye contact, "the cost is too great. Now please, follow me." He gestured forwards, through the bookcases.

Erde and Troyes followed Waren, neither feeling particularly at ease with the demons nearby. The tentacle-faced monstrosities ignored the men walking the floor. Waren led his friends through the network of aisles, staircases and walkways throughout the giant room.

He guided them outside into a small rooftop garden. Erde could see the city beneath them, realising that they had been transported to an otherwise inaccessible part of the mountain where the library sat. It was beautiful from this height, but the horrors that lay within refused to let Erde enjoy the sight. He glanced at Troyes and realised that he could see only fog.

Waren held up his hand to stop his friends from following, then disappeared behind a large wall. "Master Leer, I have brought them. May we enter your corridor?"

"They may stand before me," croaked a sickly voice.

The men rounded the corner and before them, embedded in the wall was a large face. The face's features were contorted and exaggerated, twisting and wrinkling across it. The eyes were present, but dark and empty as though nothing human lay behind them. The skin of the face stretched and merged with the wall, veins connecting to the brickwork as though they were truly one.

"I am Leer the Wall Sage," croaked the face. "Why did you seek out this library?"

Erde answered. "In truth, I only sought to find this library on the advice of the Man with Four Faces. Knowing that Waren is here, alive and well, I am happy to depart soon and leave this place undisturbed."

"Surely you would not offend me so? You come all this way and seek no knowledge?"

"I have many questions, but only two of them are truly important to me."

"Ask, and I shall answer. I know everything within this city. I have lived here since near the beginning, far longer than even Xantem has been here."

Erde appreciated the directness of Leer. "How do we leave the Necropolis? The door we entered through is sealed, the skeletal hands unwilling to open it."

"That door is not sealed forever; it is simply locked," said Leer, his face turning into a wicked scowl. "The key is to offer the door a willingly given heart. Cutting it from a foe will not suffice, you must have permission from whoever is sacrificing their life to let you escape."

Troyes spoke up. "One of us must die for the other to leave?"

Leer smiled an ugly smile. "It is as I said. Any heart, willingly given, must be presented to the door. The necromancers made it so as assurance that there would always be fresh bodies left behind. For every two that enter, at least one must die for the other to leave. A wicked method, but it has proven effective."

Waren nodded, it was evidently not new information to him. Erde and Troyes looked at each other, knowing what it would mean should they find Fueur alive.

Leer broke the silence, growing impatient. "I am a wise sage, but my time is valuable, even in a place where I am eternal. What is your other question?"

"We're seeking our band's leader, Fueur," said Erde. "Do you know where he is?"

Waren looked away as Leer answered. "The man seeking to cure his dreaded sickness is enshrined in metal and fire. He walks the city as the Ash Knight. Xantem the Black granted his wish at a cost far greater than your leader could have imagined."

Erde turned to Troyes. "What sickness?" Troyes shrugged with a look of visible confusion before turning towards Waren.

The sorcerer answered. "Fueur had intense headaches and seizures. He hid them from everyone, even his own sister. I was the only one who knew, and only after finding him collapsed on the floor one evening. They had been growing worse and we could not find a priest able to heal him, so he sought the Necropolis. It was long rumoured to possess the Elixir of Life that could cure any malady, but it was not true."

Troyes nodded his head. "You encouraged us to follow him because you felt guilty for sending him towards a rumour."

"I wrestled with the decision, but I realised that it was foolish of me to give him false hope. I may not have realised it was false hope at the time, yet it is my fault that he is damned. I will stay here in the Necropolis as punishment, aiding Master Leer with whatever tasks he assigns me. It will be my penance until my dying day. A day that will not come naturally, as is the nature of Furcht."

Erde stepped towards Leer who scrunched his nose up. "Master Leer, can you tell me if Fueur is alive or dead? Is there any way he be saved or are we too late?"

Leer smiled again. "He is somewhere between life and death, yet not fully undead...for now. Xantem's power is great and you will not be able to break the snare that he has placed upon your leader. The lich is both priest and sorcerer, powered by the roots of evil and the branches of death. If you want to stand a hope of defending yourself, then you will require the aid of Kleve the Smith King."

"Who is this Smith King?" asked Troyes, hoping he could be provided with a weapon better suited to slaying the monsters of this place.

"The last of the giants in this land, descended from the northern giants that survived the ending of the Dawn Era. He is a man focused on his craft beyond all else, and his craft is truly something to marvel at."

Erde nodded. "We will seek him if you tell us where to find him."

Leer began to cough and splutter. "I grow tired...and weak. Waren, send in one of my servants to tend to me.'"

"At once, Master Leer," said Waren as he walked away.

"What is it that ails you?" asked Troyes.

Leer let out a deep laugh that turned into a coughing fit. "There are many illnesses in this world, both mundane and magical. I am afraid that mine goes beyond even that. I have a sickness of the soul that cannot be mended, yet this place prevents it from getting worse."

"That didn't answer me question," said Troyes, not one to care for riddles.

Leer grimaced. "I am a sorcerer, barbarian. A brilliant sorcerer, capable of bending the demons in the library to my will. It is a great power, but sorcery takes a heavy toll on you. I was on the verge of death before being drawn into the city many centuries ago. Now, I linger on, bound to the walls. The only way for my malady to be kept at bay outside of this realm is held by the Outer World god, Carmathus, but he would never aid me."

Erde had never heard of this Outer World god and didn't care enough to ask. Waren returned and informed Leer that one of the servants would be with him shortly.

"Thank you, Waren," he said, before his eyes fell upon Erde and Troyes once more. "You are welcome to stay a while in my library, but please leave me to rest now. My apprentice can instruct you on where to find Kleve."

"Rest well, Master Leer," said Waren, taking a bow. "I will reconvene with you in the morning and share what I have learned from my studies."

The three men walked back inside and Waren led them back to the ground floor. There were few words exchanged during the climb down. The sorcerer led them to a large desk and gestured for his friends to sit. Erde and Troyes both sat, still nervously eyeing the robed librarian demons.

"Do not mind the bibliographers," said Waren. "It is as I said before, they will not harm you without cause. Master Leer has full control over them. If you do not interfere with their work, they will leave you alone. Interfering with their work is a great disruption to Master Leer."

"Interfere?" asked Erde, suspecting that he already knew the answer.

"Do not touch the books, do not touch them and do not get in their way. They are doing important work that should not be disturbed."

"What work are they doing?"

"I would explain it to you, Erde, but I am afraid that it was a struggle for even I to understand at first. I am afraid that it would not be a good use of time to explain it to you."

Erde was irked at the comment, yet he was pleased to see that Waren had not changed one bit since he arrived here. The man was as socially inept as ever.

Troyes leaned forwards in his chair. "Surely there must be another way to leave this place? A willingly-given heart? Are we supposed to cut each other's hearts out?" He laughed at the preposterousness of the notion, but trailed off rather sadly.

Waren nodded. "Unfortunately for anybody who comes here, that's the idea. Unless you have the power to rip holes between the planes, then that is the only way. The creators of this realm were many and they were powerful."

"And twisted," added Troyes.

"There is that too, yes. Even Xantem himself cannot leave here without a heart, not that he would want to. He is a descendent of the original necromancers who built Furcht and, while more powerful than us, is vastly inferior to their collective powers. The magic that sustains this place is old and powerful."

Troyes grinned a toothy grin. "Go back to the part where you speak of his inferiority. I like the word inferior when speaking of my enemies. I look forward to crushing his head with my foot." Troyes leaned back in his chair and slammed his fist on the table. "If we are to stand a chance of freeing

Fueur from the clutches of that rotten bastard, we will need help. Who is this Kleve fellow? I don't care who he descended from; I care about what he can do for us."

Waren tapped his fingers together as he spoke. "Kleve the Smith King is a blacksmith who lives in one of the many tunnels and chambers underneath the city. This place is home to secrets hard to fathom, and Kleve's territory is one of such places. I have yet to meet him, but I know he is renowned.

"He was a legendary smith even before he arrived here and has since honed his craft, never aging and undisturbed for almost as long as Master Leer has been here. Even Xantem does not bother him, but I cannot say why he leaves him alone. What I can say is that Kleve lives in the Fire Sanctum and it's a long and dangerous journey underground to reach this lair of his."

Troyes smiled. "Surely you know us better, Waren. Erde and I do not fear danger. Give us the directions and we will reach our destination, one way or another."

"It is precisely because I know your capabilities that I believe you will die on the way," said Waren. "There are beings beyond your comprehension that guard the path. Many are the undead experiments of Xantem, others are the experiments of his predecessors. Only a handful of individuals in the history of the Necropolis have reached Kleve through legitimate means."

"Stop dropping hints and tell me of the illegitimate means," demanded Troyes, slamming his fist on the table.

Waren sighed. "This library contains a portal to a pocket dimension, where you can find doors to anywhere in this city. The being that lives there is more deadly than any on the journey to the Fire Sanctum, but that being is one...not many. The Void Worm. It's so powerful that I believe it can transcend the Necropolis and venture back to the real world should it choose to. It comes from beyond the Outer World and is a horror greater than any you have seen before, Troyes."

"An unimportant matter. It is as you said, this Void Worm is one foe rather than many. That's the way we will go, right Erde?" asked Troyes.

Neither Troyes nor Waren had realised that Erde had fallen asleep minutes ago.

*

The following day, Waren led Erde and Troyes through the library and into a small chamber on the fifth floor. The chamber was empty save for a single portal on the far wall. It swirled and hummed, asking the men to venture into its mysterious destination.

"Are you sure you won't come with us?" Erde asked Waren.

"I am certain. I am not a strong man and cannot be relied upon in battle."

"Your magic is great," insisted Erde.

"My magic is merely acceptable, but I appreciate your words. No, I will only slow you down should you need to run...and you will need to run."

Troyes glanced at Waren. "Remind me of the symbol to look for on the door."

Waren frowned and removed a piece of parchment from his dark robes. He ignited his finger in fire, then extinguished it, leaving it blackened. He drew an ornate symbol with sharp lines that Erde would best describe as resembling an overly complex furnace. He showed the parchment to Troyes before handing it to Erde for safekeeping.

"Good luck, my friends," said Waren, extending a hand. "Should we never meet again, I will remember you both centuries from now."

Erde clasped Waren's hand and slapped his back. "I hope we do meet again, Waren."

Troyes gave Waren a salute, which was sincerely returned. They were never particularly close, often clashing over their vastly different personalities, but they had always been able to rely on each other in and out of battle.

Erde and Troyes walked through the portal, one after another, and were dragged from the library and spat out into a realm as bizarre as Waren has described. The portal behind them was now replaced by a door with a bookshelf symbol in the same ornate style that Waren had drawn the Fire Sanctum symbol.

The large room they were in was connected to various other rooms by staircases and archways. What made this most bizarre was that the staircases crept up the ceiling and across the roof. The archways themselves embedded all six surfaces of the room. It was dizzying to look at.

Erde walked over to one of the staircases that connected the floor to the wall and started walking. The first few steps were normal but gradually rotated until they were one with the wall. Erde reached the end of the stairs and looked at Troyes, now standing on the wall from Erde's perspective.

"I hate this place," spat Troyes, a man who preferred simplicity. "We should have taken the deadly route."

"Keep an eye out for the Void Worm," warned Erde as Troyes followed him in defying gravity.

"How can I keep an eye out when I don't know which way is up and which way is down?"

The duo walked through a series of rooms, sometimes walking on the walls, sometimes on the ceiling and sometimes on the ground. It didn't take long, but they had lost track of which was which at this point. When Erde thought about it, he realised the door to the library may not even have left them the right way up.

There was an eerie silence in the air. At least in the city, the occasional rumble of a ghoul or drip of water gave an indication of life. This dimension was void of all, both living and dead.

The men walked for what could have been hours, checking each door they found. There were symbols, some with a more obvious meaning than others. Erde was confident that one of the doors led to the shrine of V'andrya that he had set ablaze, whereas others looked like messy squiggles.

A guttural squelch echoed throughout the strange dimension; its origin unclear. Erde and Troyes looked in opposite directions, each of them certain they knew where it had come from.

"The Void Worm knows we're here," said Erde, to which Troyes nodded slowly in agreement.

The outlander was still trying to determine the source of the noise. The duo quickly decided that it did not matter. They must pick up the pace of their search or risk encountering the cosmic horror inhabiting this confusing abyss.

The pair began to run, leaping up steps and hurrying from door to door, trying to match the symbol on the parchment to the one on the door. The frustration was growing as the echoing sound grew closer. The worm was hunting them. It wanted them gone from its domain, one way or another.

A shadowy form passed quickly overhead, too quickly for either mercenary to see. The swordsman and the outlander stopped, raising their weapons in case the Void Worm was capable of defying the rules of this plane. Its echoey squelch lingered in the air, long after the shadow had vanished.

"Left," called Erde as a shadow passed by once more.

It was much closer this time but had vanished before Troyes could see it. The men waited, facing in opposite directions. The creature was too close and too fast for them to risk searching more doors. No, they must face it.

"There!" called Troyes, as the Void Worm burst from an archway in front of him.

Erde spun round to see it hurtling through the air towards them. It was black as night with six large purple orbs on what may or may not have been its face. A large void sat at the centre of the orbs, perhaps the mouth it was planning to devour them with. It radiated a violet glow and left streams of vapour in its wake that vanished into the air seconds later.

The two men leapt aside, Troyes swinging around to slash its sleek body with his rusty sword.

No sooner had a wound been torn open, than it oozed more vapour and repaired itself. The worm disappeared through one of the archways ahead, continuing to echo.

"It's too big to turn. Follow it and keep searching," ordered Erde.

The duo ran through the arch and checked for doors with little luck. Suddenly, the Void Worm burst from the side and narrowly missed Erde. He felt an intense burning on his right arm where the worm's vapour had touched him. His arm looked to be unharmed, but it was an unwelcome sensation.

The men continued to search, growing more desperate and frustrated with each door they checked. There were tens of thousands of doors in the city, and they had not even searched a thousand doors yet.

Each new path led to new doors, and the worm continued to dart from room to room, aiming to ingest them. They slashed at it, stabbed it, and had a few narrow misses, but it was not slowed down nor was it showing any sign of tiring.

"That's it," said Erde, pointing to a door on the ceiling. The two charged up the staircases, trying to navigate the maze leading towards the door.

They were within seconds of reaching the door when the Void Worm burst from the ceiling, aiming straight for Erde. Troyes shoved him out of the way and was grabbed by the otherworldly beast.

"Go!" yelled Troyes, his lower half caught inside the worm's mouth. He was struggling to pull himself free, as the worm sped through another archway.

Erde did not hesitate and pulled open the door. He leapt through the portal it hid and was dragged through the vortex, away from the labyrinthian realm.

Chapter 9

The Fire Sanctum

Erde fell to the ground. The heat of the Fire Sanctum was intense, Erde could barely breathe as he struggled to his feet. The large cavern had a reddish tint and the stone floor was of fine grey brick.

The room was crackling with fire and the loud clank of a giant man beating his giant hammer against metal. Standing at least thirty feet tall was Kleve, working on his weapons at a huge forge. The room was lined with thousands of his works, small and large, from daggers to pauldrons.

Kleve himself wore metal armour that covered his legs, torso and shoulders. The skin on his arms was burned and scarred while his face was obscured by a large helmet that rose into two twisted horns.

"What?" asked Kleve, not looking up from his work.

"Master Smith, my name is Erde of Olfen," said Erde. "I need a weapon, one that is capable of facing the Void Worm."

"Such a weapon is beyond my powers," said Kleve, continuing to hammer. "A being of cosmic nature is no match for weapons of the physical realm, even magically enhanced weapons."

"Is there anything that can stand against such a beast?"

"I can give you a suit of armour that can withstand its essence for a short period of time. It is an armour far more powerful than any armour found within this entire city, and many cities even in the Outer World."

Erde nodded. "Yes, Master Smith, I will take it."

Kleve stopped hammering and walked over to Erde, standing over him at least six times his height. "Take it? No, you can buy it. I do not give such power for free."

"I only have my silver and this sword," said Erde, showing him Sabrae's Leg.

"That sword is inferior to my craftmanship," spat Kleve. "Do not insult me. You will have to offer me something more valuable."

"What will you accept?" asked Erde, with nothing left to give.

Kleve crouched in front of Erde and prodded him in the chest with a finger the length of Erde's arm. "Your remaining years."

"If it is a fight you want, I will oblige," said Erde, readying himself.

"No, you fool," shouted Kleve, growing

impatient. "I will take seven years of your remaining natural lifespan as payment. If you die in battle before that, then it is of no consequence to you. If you are destined to die from old age, you will die seven years earlier. Take it or leave it."

"I will take your deal," said Erde without hesitation.

Kleve turned his back on Erde and walked back to his forge, continuing to hammer once more. It was as though the conversation had never happened.

"Do not ignore me," said Erde. "What of the armour?"

"I will finish my work first, then begin. If you want to snoop about my sanctum and browse my creations, I will not stop you. If you try and take anything without my permission, I will use your body as fuel for the forge."

"You do not understand," insisted Erde. "My friend is trapped in the Void Worm's realm. Trapped in the beast's mouth, no less. I cannot let him die because I'm waiting here."

"My time does not revolve around your schedule, human. I am the one who is doing you a favour, lest you forget. I sympathise with your plight, but the outcome is of no consequence to me."

Erde was furious but could see that he was out of options. He stood and waited for Kleve to set aside his latest sword, wondering if Troyes was already dead.

"Fancy seeing you here," said the Man with Four Faces. "You seem to be waiting for me wherever I go."

Erde turned and saw the golden wanderer,

bearing his happy face, approaching from a giant archway in the cavern wall. He was carelessly swinging his bloodstained mace around. Erde suspected that he must have taken the long way down.

"Why do you continue to follow me?" asked Erde.

"I am visiting my friend, Kleve," said the man, his helmet switching to the neutral face. "Did you know he forged me this fine helmet? He bolstered this old mace of mine too."

"What did it cost you?"

"Twelve years, none of which matter as we do not age in the Necropolis. If I were to leave, I'm sure I would care a lot more."

"You don't intend on leaving?"

"I see no need. My name is probably long-forgotten and my loved ones will all be dead by now."

"I'm very sorry to hear that," muttered Erde.

"You do not need to be. It no longer makes me sad. My memories of them remain and I will treasure them until I die and am reunited with them. Do you have children, stranger?"

"My name is Erde," said the mercenary, introducing himself to the man at last. "Yes, I have two children. Twins, in fact. My son Josef and my daughter Marta."

"I trust that they're both still alive, Erde? They're at home with their mother?"

Erde hesitated before answering. "Their mother is recently deceased."

The man paused for a moment before his helmet suddenly turned to the sad face. "The lust demons?"

Erde nodded, confirming the man's suspicions.

"I did not know that she was your wife. My sympathies are greater than ever. I suggest that you value your life and escape. Do not die here and leave your children parentless, even if you believe you are doing what's best for them. My son's time was all too short, and I was stuck in here trying to find a cure for his illness. In doing so, I missed his final weeks."

"Illness? That's what Fueur came for. He was sick and only Waren knew."

The man's face turned neutral. "A few come here with good intentions, others come for treasures, and others come because they cannot accept what is meant to be. Your friend and I have that in common. We both linger on here in different ways. Alive, but not living."

"You know how to leave this place. Is that why you pushed me towards the library?"

"That, and I knew that one of your companions was there. I was growing tired of my question-and-answer game. I thought a nudge in the right direction was the right thing to do."

"I appreciate it, sincerely," said Erde.

The man gave a courteous nod as his helmet spun, landing on his happy face. "You are most welcome."

"There is no way I can convince you to leave with us to return to the real world?"

"I do not see the point. There is nothing left for me there. I have accepted that my role is to help others escape from this place. I do not want another to die so that I may live in the Outer World alone."

Erde nodded. "If that is your wish, I will respect

it."

The two men stood quietly as the beating of metal on metal continued. Kleve stopped and dipped his sword in a large barrel of water.

"I am finished for now," said Kleve, at last. "Approach, impatient one."

"I shall take my leave," bowed the Man with Four Faces. "Farewell, Erde. Farewell, Kleve."

"Farewell, Alrich," said Kleve, as the man walked through the archway. "You are welcome to stay longer next time."

"Alrich?" asked Erde.

"That is indeed my real name," said the man without looking back.

Erde had told the man his name but forgotten to ask him his. Alrich. The same name as the King of Kalmere who disappeared a few decades ago. A coincidence, surely?

The mercenary stood in front of Kleve, who eyed him up. "Yes, the armour should fit with minimal adjustments. You are the perfect height, which makes things easier."

Kleve took five strides and crossed the cavern. He reached down, brushed aside a pile of cuirasses, and grabbed a small trunk. He dropped it in front of Erde and asked him to open it.

The armour inside was made of a black metal. It was shaped with ridges and grooves that resembled bones, giving it a skeletal look.

"I call it the black skull armour. It is made from Kalt steel, infused with black augurite from the deep. The bones are from long-dead necromancers that I have combined with the metal. There is one thing it still needs to activate its true power, but you must first put it on."

Erde hastily armoured up, not wanting to waste any more time. As he placed the helmet on his head, Kleve grabbed him. Erde tried to break free as Kleve raised his hammer and bashed him with it.

Much to Erde's surprise, he felt no pain. He did, however, feel briefly ill. It was a strange sensation, but seconds later he was fine. At the same time, the armour reshaped itself into a perfect fit for Erde.

Kleve laughed, sensing the look on Erde's concealed face. "That was the feeling of losing seven years. Three years infused into the armour and four years are given to me as payment. Anybody who wears the armour while it contains your life force will wear it as normal steel. While it is adorning your flesh, it is near impenetrable."

"Thank you, Master Smith," said Erde, saluting.

"If you choose to return the armour, I will give you three years of your life back, but I make no demands for it back. You can keep it until you die if you so wish."

"How do I return to the Void Worm's dimension? I do not see the portal."

"There is no portal from this side," said Kleve.

"How can this be?" asked Erde, incredulously.

"One more year and I can make the portal appear for you."

"Fine, take it."

"You should be less reckless with your life. Is it not precious to you?"

"Perhaps you can stop asking me for my life when I am trying to save the life of another? Is life not precious to you or is it only your own?"

"Very well," said Kleve, bowing his head in shame. "I will take only half a year this time, and use half a year from what you have already given me."

Kleve hit Erde with the hammer once more, then slammed it on the floor. The portal materialised on the stone as the giant raised his hammer. Erde wasted no time jumping into the hypnotic swirl.

He jolted through the hole in space and landed on his feet in the warped realm of the worm. Its squelch echoed once more. It was angry. Troyes must still be alive.

Erde sprinted from room to room, through the archways and up and down the staircases. He followed the terrifying sound of the Void Worm until he finally saw it in one of the larger rooms.

Troyes sat atop the worm, his skin red and raw from the vapour burns, clutching his sword and trying to stab the creature. Each time he pulled his sword free, the wound healed just as he struck again. The Void Worm, whatever it was, was seemingly immortal.

Erde charged forwards and caught the worm's attention. The beast made for the armoured swordsman, the outlander still clinging to its back. Erde held out Sabrae's Leg, pointing it to the ground.

The Void Worm tried to devour him, but the black skull armour left him unscathed. The worm's lower half was split in two as it charged into the sword, the creature unfolding like a blanket. Its unholy screech echoed throughout the room, as Troyes fell from the top of the monster.

Erde rushed over to his friend. He was unconscious but breathing. The worm's vapour had burned him badly. Erde picked up his friend as the Void Worm began to rise up.

Its wound repaired itself, stitching the worm back together. It flew through an archway ahead, seeking the space to change direction and attack the two invaders once more. Its assault was unrelenting and the beast was not tired. Not even being split in half would slow it down.

Granting its wish for them to leave, Erde rammed into the nearest door and straight through the portal on the other side. He landed unstably on the stone tiles, then immediately fell forward upon a set of steps that lay in front of him.

He collected himself and hoisted Troyes over his shoulder once more. Erde knew this place. He had emerged from the catacombs in the Cathedral of the True One.

The mercenary marched up the steps and laid his friend on the nearest pew to rest. "I'm sorry that I was not faster, Troyes," muttered Erde.

"Urgh..." grunted Troyes, half-conscious and unable to give a more coherent response.

Erde threw down his helmet and walked over to the statue of the winged angel. He dropped to his knees and prayed. He thought of his children, he thought of his dead wife, he thought of his lost leader.

He prayed that he was still comatose and would wake up from the nightmare that was the last few days. He prayed that his wife's soul would reach the Inner World. He prayed that he would find the Ash Knight again and have the strength to kill him. His last desire in Furcht was to free Fueur from his torment in this accursed plane.

Erde stood up. He placed the black skull helmet firmly on his head and walked to the doors. He must find Alrich, the Man with Four Faces. As the man had healed Erde's shoulder, he would be able to heal Troyes.

The swordsman dashed past the pews, past the staircase to the catacombs, and over to the large wooden doors. He pulled them back and stepped through the door once more, but a figure was already approaching him. A man in golden armour. The Man with Four Faces.

Chapter 10

Beneath the Square

Erde was shocked to see the Man with Four Faces approaching him. "What are you doing here? You were down in the Fire Sanctum mere minutes ago?"

"There are many doors and tunnels in this place that you discover," said Alrich. "It is simply a matter of knowing which one to take. Is your friend still alive?"

"Yes," said Erde.

He did not waste time questioning the enigmatic stranger, that could wait. He led him inside to Troyes. The outlander gritted his teeth as he lay unconscious, writhing in silent agony.

"This will hurt," warned Alrich. "Pin him down."

Erde leaned hard on Troyes' arms. As strong as Erde was, Troyes was stronger. If he wrestled too much, things would get ugly.

Alrich removed his gauntlets and placed his pale hands just above Troyes' chest. He silently focused and his hands glowed a soft, warm yellow. The ethereal burns on Troyes' skin slowly faded, but as they faded the outlander began to struggle.

"Stop moving," Erde barked at him, but Troyes could not control himself. He tried to sit up as Erde used all of his strength to hold his injured companion down.

Alrich moved his hands across the outlander's wounds, from his torso to his legs to his arms. It was when Alrich reached his face that Troyes finally opened his eyes and roared.

Troyes wrestled his arms free and grabbed Alrich, trying to end the pain. Erde wrapped an arm around his neck and pulled. It worked. Troyes released Alrich and began thumping on Erde's black gauntlets. The armour protected Erde who otherwise might have received a broken arm.

"It's done," said Alrich as he stepped back from the pew.

"Good," said Erde as he released an again-unconscious Troyes.

"You almost strangled the poor fellow. Is he alright?" asked Alrich, not wanting to come any closer.

"He will be. We'll let him rest for a while. Thank you for your help, Alrich."

"You are welcome, my friend. It would be disgraceful for me to sit idly by and let your friend succumb to the Worm."

Erde decided that now was the time for

answers. "How did you get here so fast? You were with me in Kleve's room a short while ago."

Alrich chuckled as his mask rotated. "There are many secret doors and tunnels in this place. It is simply a matter of knowing which ones to take to reach your destination. I found a new one as recently as last week."

"I do not hope to remain here for that long."

"I am sure that you will not."

"Is there any way for this place to be destroyed? What about killing Xantem?"

Alrich's face rotated to the angry expression again. "I have killed him a dozen times over when he ventures from his lair and it has only served to bring a momentary peace while he recovers."

"He cannot die?"

"He is a lich whose soul is not bound to his body. His body is merely a conduit for his being while his soul stays put somewhere hidden. It's called a phylactery."

"Where can we find this phylactery? I'll smash it into a million pieces."

"I have searched for decades and have yet to find it, but...there is something we could do."

"Tell me," said Erde, determined to get revenge on the lich who had brought him so much despair.

"There is a place here, deep underground, that houses something of great importance to Xantem. It's called the Death Tree."

"Why is it so important to him?"

Alrich shook his head. "The living do not wander to the Necropolis as much as they used to. The bodies that Xantem warps and mutilates into his monstrous creations are not plentiful so he created something truly abominable. A tree that bears not seeds, but a tree that bears the dead. It is wicked, evil magic.

"It is the Death Tree that drew the Void Worm here in the first place, sensing a strong divine power. The power of an Inner World god, the power of Mallabeth. The Death Tree is an extension of Mallabeth, manifested through Xantem's darkly divine magic. It is the lifeblood of the Necropolis. One piece of the puzzle that can turn this hollow city to ash."

"If we destroy the tree, he cannot create new undead?"

"Not unless more unfortunate souls arrive in Furcht. I know the route to the tree, but I cannot destroy it alone. The dead are too numerous and I am forced to retreat each time."

"And he cannot create a new tree?"

"For that, he needs yet more bodies."

"You are certain that it is there? How did you learn of it?"

"Leer. He knows this place better than anybody. He helped build it and is eternally bound to it, fused to the wall. Cursed for his sins."

"And Xantem? Will he be by the tree?"

"I cannot say for certain, but it is possible. It is well guarded so I would suspect he wants the same protection."

"Troyes and I will get you to the tree," said Erde confidently. "We will help you destroy it."

Alrich's helmet rotated to the happy face.

*

Troyes awoke in the middle of the night in a groggy state, remembering very little from his tussle with the Void Worm. After he had had been filled in on what had happened and the plan to destroy the Death Tree, he was alert and brimming with enthusiasm once more.

When the sun had risen, the three men departed from the safety of the Cathedral of the True One and headed towards the town square. Alrich had assured them that what they sought lay there.

"I have passed here many times over now. How did I not see it?" asked Erde as they approached the fountain. The statue of the man holding the egg loomed overhead.

"Do you remember what I told you about secret doors and tunnels?" asked Alrich.

Erde did not answer. He knew that Alrich was the expert on Furcht by many miles. Questioning him seemed stupid, so he trusted in the Man with Four Faces to steer them right.

The fountain on the other side of the passageway was filled with residue and grime, but this version of the fountain was empty. Erde wondered how the real world differed from this pocket plane and what secrets this one held that the other did not.

Alrich stepped onto the ledge and hopped inside the fountain base. Erde and Troyes watched as he stepped on the pedestal, grabbed the stone egg and twisted it. The ground rumbled as the base of the fountain began to break apart and descend into a circular stone staircase.

"How many undead are waiting for us down here?" asked Troyes, as he climbed into the staircase.

"At least a hundred and a variety of different types," said Alrich nonchalantly. "They grow on trees, you know."

The three men laughed as they began the descent into the bowels of Furcht. As the light began to fade, Erde lit a torch he had taken from the cathedral and Alrich cast the Orb of Light spell. Troyes remarked that his vision was good enough without a light to aid him.

"Is this also the way to Kleve?" asked Erde.

Alrich shook his head. "No, he's closer to the cathedral. There are many underground tunnels and pits in this city. I wouldn't be surprised if some of them went so deep that they were at the bottom edge of the Outer World."

"If this place still counts as the Outer World," said Erde.

"Yes, there is that to consider," admitted Alrich. "Although the fact that sorcery and divine magic still works suggests that it is on some level. A much stronger connection than that between the Outer World and Inner World."

The walk down the staircase seemed endless, but nobody complained. After what felt like an hour, they emerged into a tunnel. There were no undead to be seen, but Alrich was certain that they were getting close.

He led the way, followed by Troyes and then Erde. Troyes had insisted on taking the rear, but Erde refused to allow him. "Your armour is in tatters and you have only just recovered from your injuries," he said.

The tunnels were winding, but they grew increasingly wide as the men walked along. Alrich held up his hand, signalling for the mercenaries to stop. He dissipated his orb and Erde put out his torch. Alrich pointed towards a heaving human-shaped silhouette, surrounded by a soft orange glow from crystals embedded in the walls.

Erde and Troyes drew their swords while Alrich readied his mace. They moved slowly forwards, but the figure only grew larger as they approached. What had seemed the shape and size of a regular man from the distant blurry darkness revealed itself to be a skeleton that was three times as large. Erde was immediately reminded of the giant skeleton in the catacombs.

The creature turned towards them as they approached and took giant strides in their direction. The men unleashed hell upon the skeletal behemoth, quickly breaking its legs and bringing it to the ground in a rain of bones.

"There will be more nearby," warned Alrich. "This is where the real fighting begins."

"I welcome it," said Troyes.

Troyes pushed his way to the front, leading the way deeper. He would not hear any arguments otherwise now that they could see the way ahead thanks to the faint orange light from the cavern crystals.

"Here come more," said Troyes as he charged at a gathering of three of the giant skeletons. Erde and Alrich rushed to join him, each taking on a skeleton of their own.

The tunnels here were wider, but it was a cramped space to fight giants in. Luckily for the men, the skeletons had a more difficult time and collided with each other in the chaos. All three fell before long, leaving a mountain of bones where they once stood.

"Are these giant skeletons related to Kleve?" asked Erde.

"I do not honestly know," said Alrich. "They are considerably smaller than he is, but giants would not be my area of expertise. I doubt that he would tell me even if I were to ask him very directly."

"How did he come to be here?"

"The same way that we all do. He sought long life, but he sought it to perfect his craft. He trades in life force, as you very well know. Little pieces of your soul sold to him, but not as you would sell to a demon. Life magic is a force more complex than you can possibly imagine."

"We can discuss the giant smith later," said Troyes, longing to break more bones.

"Lead the way," said Alrich, gesturing ahead with his mace.

The men fought their way through more sections of the tunnels, the undead growing each minute. They came in all shapes and sizes, some with flesh, some without. Many had a single head, others had multiple.

First, they fought seven of them, then they fought eleven of them, then sixteen, then twenty-five. All three were growing tired and Alrich seized quiet moments to tend to their injuries with his divine magic.

"How much further do we have to go?" asked Erde as he shattered a shin, bringing a large two-headed ghoul to its knees.

"We are not far," said Alrich, casting his Freeze Undead spell on one of his foes while parrying a thump from a giant boney fist. "This is the furthest I have been."

The warriors continued to fight, refusing to retreat. They had come so far and could not afford to back down and let the dead rise again. No, this was their chance and they would seize it.

As they defeated another dozen of Xantem's minions, they rounded a corner into another long tunnel. An army of the undead stretched out before them, each already moving towards the trio menacingly. There must have been at least a hundred.

"Do you see the opening ahead?" asked Alrich, turning to Erde. "I am going to handle these worthless peons while the two of you run as fast as you can. The Death Tree should be in the next cavern. Do you understand?"

"We are not leaving you here," said Erde, striking the first skeleton to reach them.

"If I am still alive when you return, you can help me then. The last thing we want is more undead from the tree joining this army."

"I will stay," said Troyes. "You are nimbler than me and that armour of yours will protect you up ahead. We can draw their attention here while you burn that tree to the ground."

Erde did not like the plan. "I can make it through, but I cannot let you face these brutes alone. There are far too many of them."

"If you want to help destroy this place then you must destroy the tree," insisted Alrich as he froze a giant in place.

He was right. "I will do it," relented Erde.

"Go!" yelled Troyes as he threw a smaller skeleton against the tunnel wall. "I will follow and distract them near the exit."

Erde took one last look at Alrich before dashing

through the horde. The gallant warrior's helmet rested on his angry face as he smashed skeletons apart.

The two mercenaries took out as many as they could along the way. As the pair neared the end of the tunnel, Troyes stopped and yelled a battle cry to draw attention away from Erde. The skeletons began to swarm the outlander and Erde bolted through the opening.

He emerged into the huge cavern and stopped dead in his tracks. It was here. It loomed over him, at least fifty feet tall, with roots that plunged to the bottom of the world and branches that cast shadows over the entire room, each bearing a dozen corpses that dangled on cords of flesh. The Death Tree.

It reflected a soft orange light from the crystals that covered the walls. At the base of the tree was a throne of skulls where a figure clad in purple robes and a golden crown sat. Standing by his side was a knight in ashen armour.

Chapter 11

The Death Tree

Xantem the Black and the Ash Knight watched Erde approach. As he had expected, being tackled off a cliff would not keep a lich's thrall down for long. The evil lich with the black skull sat on his throne, his hand on a gnarled wooden staff made from the branches of the tree above him.

The Death Tree made the terrifying sight of these two powerful foes all the more intimidating. Erde was not powerful enough to defeat the Ash Knight alone, never mind paired with his undead master. No, he would need to find a way to attack the tree while staying alive.

"I did not think that you would dare venture this far, Erde of Olfen," said Xantem.

Erde said nothing as he walked towards the

centre of the room.

"You will answer me when I speak to you, human. Perhaps if you show respect I will treat you more favourably and torture you just a little bit less before killing you."

It was impossible for Erde to read the fleshless monstrosity that sat before him. "You are not worthy of respect, lich. You will release Fueur at once. You will let us leave this place and perhaps you will survive to see tomorrow."

Xantem cackled erratically. "You are as bold as I was told, and equally as stupid. You are in my domain and you cannot make threats here. I am all-powerful and you are but a man in a suit of metal and bone wielding the bitch spider's leg. You are nothing here and in this realm I am more powerful than the True One. You will learn your place one way or another."

"You think that you are all-powerful, but I will make you see that it is mere illusion. A fantasy in your own head. This realm, whatever parallel pocket of existence it is, is a façade. In the real world, even the dogs would spit on you."

Xantem leaned forward and pointed his staff at Erde. "You forget something crucial, mercenary. We are not in the real world...are we?" He swung his staff upwards, and the Ash Knight stirred.

Erde held Sabrae's Leg high and readied himself for the fight of his life as Fueur stepped forth with his own molten blade glowing hot.

"Fueur," called Erde. "I will put an end to the evil spell and set your soul free. It is not too late for you to be saved. Lay down your sword and join me against Xantem."

Fueur stopped but did not put down his sword.

He assumed a defensive stance, once again waiting for his opponent to strike first. Erde walked towards him and stopped twenty feet in front of him, mirroring the Ash Knight's position.

"Come at me," said Erde. "Strike me first."

The two swordsmen faced each other, neither making a move. Erde could hear the fight between Alrich, Troyes and the undead raging behind him. Xantem merely sat and watched from his throne.

"Strike me!" yelled Erde.

Much to his surprise, the Ash Knight charged forwards and struck first. Erde parried with his sword, but the knight kicked him to the ground. Erde rolled backwards and shot to his feet as Fueur lunged at him, striking his black skull armour. The plate was indeed strong, not taking a scratch. The Ash Knight did not expect this, giving Erde the chance to strike his leg. He buckled and Erde shoved him to the ground, then followed up with a blow to the head.

The knight barely noticed the strike and rolled aside. He sprung to his feet and charged forward again. The two men traded blows, the Ash Knight with a considerable speed advantage in spite of his much heftier greatsword.

Erde did not have Troyes with him to take half of the knight's attention this time. Kleve's armour was the only reason he was still alive. The swordsman knew he was losing, but he would not stop. If he should die today, it would be on his feet.

"I know you can hear me, Fueur. Fight him," said Erde, unwilling to give up on his friend.

The Ash Knight distracted Erde with a strike to the left leg, then punched him in the jaw. The helmet protected Erde, but his head spun around and he could not keep his eyes on the enemy. The Ash Knight swept the swordsman's leg and knocked him to the ground.

Erde parried the knight's attempt to impale him. He quickly drew his knife and hurled it at the knight's helmet, rolling away and climbing to his feet when Fueur blocked.

"Fueur!" yelled Troyes, bursting from the opening to the tunnel. He was bloodied and bruised, but alive.

The Ash Knight looked towards the approaching outlander. Erde saw his opening. He swung Sabrae's Leg upwards, hacking off Fueur's arm. A burst of flame shot from the opening and ashes scattered through the air. There was very little flesh and bone left. Erde backed off, expecting a counterblow, but the knight dropped his sword and fell to his knees.

Troyes limped towards the pair; his face contorted in pain with each movement. "Is he alive?"

Erde was impressed by his friend's resilience. He nodded slowly. "Yes, but we are not alone here."

Xantem watched as Troyes cautiously approached the knight and lifted his grill. Flames crackled intensely and the smell of burning flesh was unmistakable. The Ash Knight's breathing was suddenly very laboured.

He screamed in Fueur's voice, barely able to get a word out. "He...will kill you...run!"

Suddenly, Xantem vanished from his throne in a puff of smoke. A black vortex materialised on the stone floor and Xantem arose from it, levitating above the ground.

"Xantem, release Fueur at once," demanded Erde.

The lich cackled erratically. "No," he said.

Troyes, in a surprising burst of speed, leapt at the lich with his sword overhead, aiming straight for his skull. Xantem cast a flash of fire that threw Troyes backwards.

He turned and waved his staff at Erde. The swordsman could feel the lich trying to control the bones in his armour. Had Kleve given him this so that he could not stand against Xantem? Had he been betrayed?

"You will serve me as the Skull Knight," said Xantem. "What fortune that you are in a cage, ready to be enslaved."

"I will never serve you," said Erde defiantly.

"You do not have a choice. You don an armour of bone to fight against the most powerful necromancer in existence? You are a fool."

Erde gripped his sword tightly, still able to move his hand. His life force powering the armour had rendered Xantem unable to control it, and the wicked lich had not noticed.

The swordsman charged at the lich, who was caught unaware. Erde cut his staff in two, then moved to stab him in the neck, but the lich conjured a forcefield around himself using his hands.

"I am more than a magical implement, you cretin," said Xantem, unable to suppress the anger in his voice. "You think that my power is in my staff? No, my power is my very being."

Erde relentlessly attacked Xantem, but the lich disappeared in a cloud of smoke and reappeared elsewhere with each hit. He was toying with Erde,

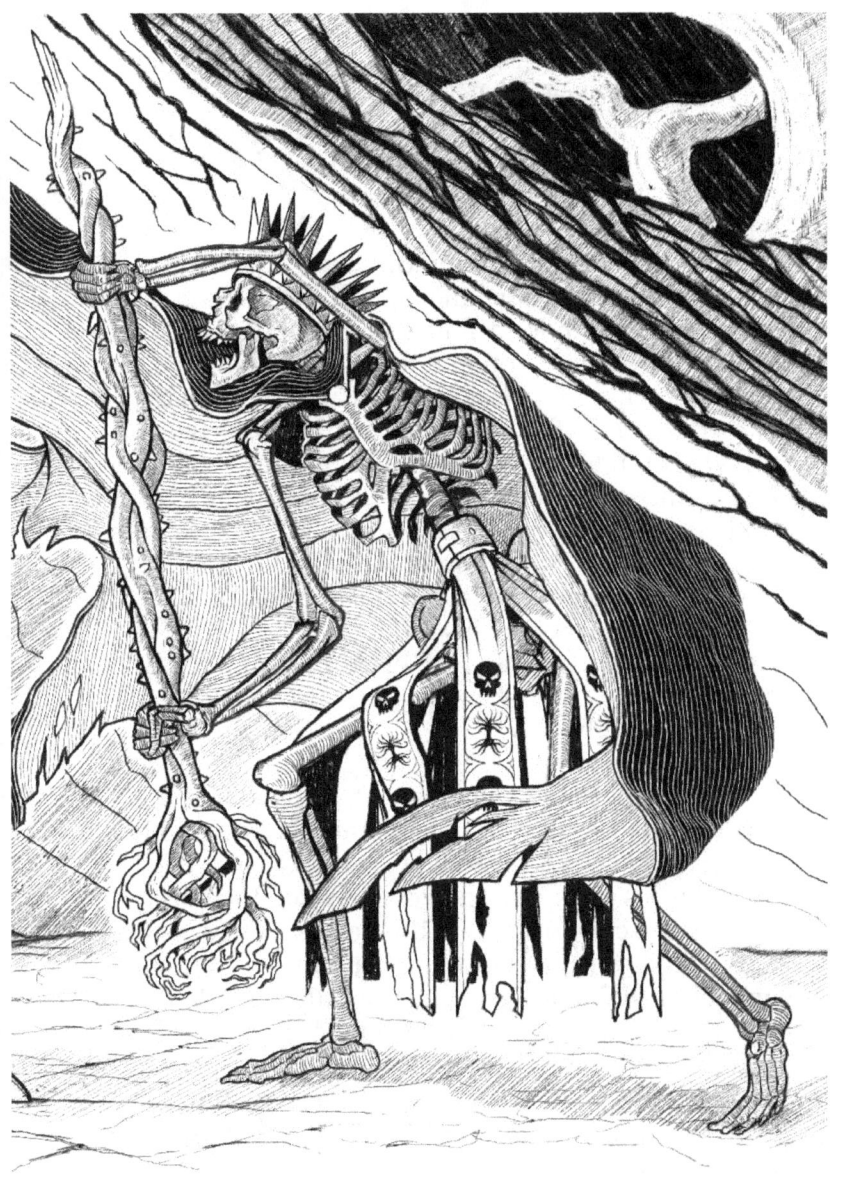

laughing the whole way.

Xantem hurled a barrage of green fireballs at Erde, but the black skull armour resisted each one. Erde shot a flurry of sparks at Xantem, who teleported away and reappeared behind. Erde predicted his movement and stabbed him in the gut.

"You do not understand," said Xantem. "I cannot be hurt. I cannot be killed." Xantem engulfed his hands in flame and grabbed Erde's helmet. He pulled it off and tossed it aside.

Xantem's spindly fingers were an inch from the swordsman's eyeballs when a towering figure threw his full weight against the lich. It was Fueur. He pinned Xantem to the ground while he desperately fought to remain himself.

Erde spotted Fueur's greatsword on the ground. Now was his chance. He ran to the molten blade and hoisted it over his shoulder. He dashed straight to the tree, drew the blade back and thrust it deep inside the rotten trunk. It was hot, but it was not enough.

The swordsman released his grip on the blade and placed both of his hands on the tree trunk. He focused all of his energy, all of his rage, and unleashed a hell storm of sparks. He yelled furiously, as the sparks flew and ignited the bark.

The tree caught fire and the flames slowly crept upwards. Erde turned just in time to see Xantem break free of Fueur's grip and raise his hands to the sky. He yelled an incantation, looking to the undead seeds hanging from the branches.

Suddenly, Xantem's body collapsed and his skull was flung across the room. Standing beside the heap of cloth and bone was Alrich, the Man with Four Faces. His mace held aloft in glory, having separated the lich from his head once again.

"I apologise for my lateness," he said, his helmet resting on his most jovial expression. "I was not so sure I would survive, yet I continue to surprise even myself."

"I too was convinced you would meet your end in that tunnel," admitted Erde. "You are more powerful than I had ever imagined."

Alrich gave a shrug. "Perhaps. Yet it was not me who set fire to the Death Tree. However, maybe sending you alone was a poor move in hindsight."

"We do not have time to rejoice for our victory or regret our errors."

"Quite right," replied Alrich. He approached Troyes and helped him to his feet, taking a moment to heal some of the outlander's more vicious wounds.

Erde rushed to Fueur's side, his brother in both law and arms now free of Xantem's influence. "Speak to me, Fueur. What can we do?"

""Cut...my heart out...flee this place," gasped Fueur, between screams. He was lucid and could feel the searing pain from the flames engulfing him beneath the Ash Knight's armour.

Erde pulled off Fueur's helmet. His face was hard to see through the fire, but his flesh was black and more ash than skin. Erde's leader continued to cry out as his body burned endlessly.

"There must be a way to save him," said Erde, desperately turning to Alrich as he helped Troyes over to his companions.

"I am truly sorry to say it, but whatever curse placed upon him is far beyond my healing capabilities," he said. "His heart, however, is being willingly offered as a means of escaping Furcht. I suggest you listen to him and take it quickly. He is your leader for a reason."

Troyes shook his head and closed his eyes, struggling to look at his dear friend.

"Do it," muttered Fueur, fighting through the pain. "Please."

Erde nodded and retrieved his knife from the ground. "May your soul leave this foul place and reach the Inner World. Tell my wife that I love her. Take care of her for me until I join you both whenever my time comes."

"Take care...of my niece...and nephew," said Fueur forcefully, pulling his fist to his chest in salute.

"Farewell, brother," said Troyes, returning the salute. Alrich joined Troyes in saluting Fueur, for once he had nothing to say.

Erde was the last to salute, his hand trembling. The swordsman raised his knife high as the former Ash Knight struggled to suppress his cries of pain. He thrust his blade into Fueur's skull, ending his torment. As Fueur's screams stopped, Erde unleashed a yell of his own. The tree burned behind him as he cut his leader's heart from his chest.

Chapter 12

Sacrificial

Erde held Fueur's charred heart in his hand as corpses rained down from the burning branches above. They landed with heavy thuds as Alrich and Troyes ran from body to body, crushing its skull. Fragments of bone sprayed through the air like rain. The undead the two men could not reach in time arose and charged towards each of the three warriors.

Erde climbed to his feet and unleashed his fury upon the undead. He was angry and wanted the remnants of Xantem's underground army destroyed. He may not be able to destroy the Necropolis, but he would bring the false Furcht to its knees. If Xantem was to return, rebuilding his army would not be an easy task.

The three men fought relentlessly as the undead continued to plummet to the ground from the crumbling Death Tree. Ashes flowed through the air like dark cherry blossoms. They swirled and danced as the undead fell one by one to the might of the heroes. The stone became a shallow lake of blood that filled with each skewering or beheading.

Erde dropped to his knees, exhausted, as the last of the undead fell. He clutched his sword in one hand and Fueur's heart in the other. It was still beating, even with the mercenary leader dead. It was waiting to be given to the door as the price of exit, kept going by the magic of the evil realm. For how long, Erde could not guess.

Troyes called over to Erde and Alrich. "Come and see." He bore a disgusted look on his face as he pointed towards the ground with his rusty blade.

All three men gathered around a black skull; a crown still firmly attached to its head. He may have been separated from his body, but Xantem the Black was not quite defeated yet.

"Do you think this makes any difference?" asked the humiliated lich. "This is my domain, forever and always. You can leave, but my work will not stop and I will never die."

"You think that you will not die one day?" asked Erde, kneeling down. "It is a fact of life that that time will come for each of us. For you it may not be today, it will not be by my hand, but I promise you that it is a day fast-approaching."

"I am going nowhere," said Alrich to the spiteful skull. "You can climb back up as many times as you like, but I will be there to bring you back down again. That is my mission in this place. I am the one who makes you feel just that little bit scared.

Isn't that right, Xantem?"

"I do not fear you, Alrich," said Xantem angrily. "I fear no man. I am the one who strikes fear into the hearts of all who come to this place."

"Shut him up," demanded Troyes. "I grow tired of his pathetic babbling."

Suddenly, a loud crunch of bone as Erde crushed Xantem's skull beneath his foot. He picked up his crown, tossed it in the air and struck it with his sword. The crown shattered and its fragments rained upon the bone-laden stone.

"How long until he gets a new body?" asked Erde, looking back towards Alrich.

"It's hard to say exactly, but there's probably a month of peace here before he returns." The Man with Four Faces scratched the metal chin on his neutral expression.

"Is there any way to find his soul?"

"I am certain that there is a way and that one day I will find it. Now that the tree is dead, I am motivated to hunt the undead once more. I had started to give up on the idea of ever being able to clear them out."

"Can we begone from this wretched place?" asked Troyes, kicking loose bones across the ground. They splashed as they landed in the blood that slowly sank into the cracks in the stone. "I would prefer not to die from a falling branch right after a victory."

Erde looked at the tree. It was falling apart with branches crashing to the ground and the trunk at a precarious angle. If he had not lost so much, he would have taken the time to bask in victory as he usually did. The three men departed from the chamber and walked through the remnants of the undead in the tunnel. The journey back up the staircase was exhausting, but nobody stopped to rest.

When they were safely back in the town square, they breathed a sigh of relief. Peace, however momentary it may be, was worth treasuring. Erde kept a solid grip on Fueur's heart, unwilling to risk anything happening to a gift as valuable as this.

"Alrich, will you see to it that Fueur's body isn't taken by Xantem when he revives? The Ash Knight should stay dead along with Fueur."

"I will," said the golden wanderer. "I will burn the body along with whatever other ghouls are here. The Pig Warden may need sliced and diced first, he's rather heavy."

"I will help you," said Troyes.

Erde knew this would happen. "We can find another heart for you."

The outlander shook his head. "No, we do not need to. I will stay here for a while and offer whatever aid I can. I would like to aid Alrich in ridding this place of Xantem's evil. Waren is here too, so I will not be alone. His expertise may be of great use, particularly in helping locate the lich's soul."

Alrich's face rotated to the happy expression. "Company that does not die within the first few hours of being here is always welcome. I will take you to my friend Kleve, he can fashion you a weapon of your choosing. He charges a heavy price, but I find that it's worth it in a land where you do not age."

"That would be good," said Troyes, twirling the rusty sword. He tossed it in the air and caught it effortlessly. "Although I must admit that I have grown fond of this ugly blade. It's sturdier than you might expect, but I think it must also be put to rest."

"If remaining here is what you want, I will respect it," said Erde to Troyes.

"I do not want it," admitted Troyes, "but it is what must be done."

Erde nodded. "Will you both accompany me to the door? I do not wish to linger in this place longer than I need to."

The three men walked through the streets northwards towards the upper mountain. Erde could see the familiar archway looming ahead and continued towards it. He stopped by the staircase and stared at the city beneath for a short while.

He saluted both men. "Thank you for your guidance, Alrich. If you are who I think you are, your name has not been forgotten in Kalmere. Your disappearance is a mystery that is talked about to this day."

Alrich's helmet displayed the happy face once again. "I do not know what you are talking about, Erde. I am a humble wanderer, nothing more and nothing less."

"Troyes. I will miss your brotherhood in battle. I know that this evil abomination of a realm will be less evil with you here to smite whatever Xantem comes up with next."

"I appreciate that, Erde," said Troyes, embracing his friend. "Perhaps we will meet again before you're old and grey. Take care of the two little ones."

"I will," said Erde, removing the shining blue amulet from around his neck. The fog returned immediately, obscuring the city from view. He threw the amulet to Troyes who caught it and fastened it around his neck.

As Erde turned to leave, a long-haired man in dark robes emerged from the thick fog. He wandered over, his head hanging lower than usual.

"You are leaving so soon?" asked Waren.

"I am surprised you came," admitted Erde. "Fueur gave his life for me to leave here, and my children will not grow up without both of their parents. I do not know how long his heart will remain beating, so I had better use it sooner rather than later."

"We will take care of things here," said Waren, kneeling before his friends and Alrich. "It was wrong of me to offer such little aid in the fight against Xantem. My penance should not be to solely serve in the library, it should be to help right the wrongs in the Necropolis. I hope you will accept both a sincere apology and an assurance that I will aid Troyes and Alrich however they should need."

Erde nodded. "I know you will, Waren. Your apology is not needed, but it is accepted. Please do not kneel before us, you are a friend."

"Thank you," said Waren, standing up straight again.

"Farewell," said Erde, giving one last salute. "May we meet again in the Outer World. I will pray for your success."

Each of the three said a last farewell to Erde as he walked down the staircase and towards the door guarded by the skeletal hands. He held out Fueur's heart as an offering, and the hands awoke once more. One hand reached for the heart, while others grabbed Erde and pulled him towards the door.

The remaining free hands opened it and threw Erde inside.

The swordsman stumbled but steadied himself. He did not look back at the door, fearful that the spell that guided him through the first time would try and lure him back inside.

Erde climbed the staircase, emerging from the darkness into the fog. The swordsman hurriedly looked around, alarmed at what he was seeing. Surely this could not be real? He had left the false, foggy Furcht.

He ran down the mountain path as fast as he could and into the ruined town. He breathed a sigh of relief upon seeing that the fog was not so thick here. It was a foggy day, that was all.

Erde laughed and removed his helmet, stashing it in his pack. He walked through the familiar ruined streets, no longer tainted by ghouls. Furcht was almost nostalgic at this point, but he had no desire to see it again anytime soon. All he wanted to see was his two children.

"Evenin'," came a gruff voice. "Did you find your friends?"

"Good evening, Garz," replied Erde, turning to face the apparition in the doorway. "I found them."

"Yet you return alone?"

"I do."

"A tale all too familiar, I'm afraid," sighed Garz. "Most do not return, but those who do usually return alone. It's been that way for as long as I've been dead."

"It was not for nought. I found the answers that I sought and did some good in my short time in the Necropolis."

Garz smiled. "I am glad to hear it. "I would have

given you more warning about what lay ahead, but you did not seem very receptive when we first met."

"No," admitted Erde, "I was unwilling to take the time to listen. It was nobody's fault but my own. Do not feel responsible for my impatience."

The two stood in silence for a while before Erde asked a question. "Why do you linger here? Are you trapped?"

"The lost souls of Furcht are all bound to the passageway. It is parallel to the Outer World, yet not quite the same. We can only move on when it is no more. I believe that it will happen eventually, but I also believe that it may be many millennia from now."

"There are those inside who want to put an end to all of it. I assure you that they will do whatever they can."

Garz chuckled. "Maybe they will get lucky, but we lost souls can't get our hopes up." The spirit looked towards the mountain path. "You should go, Erde. Before the passageway tries to call you back in."

"I will."

"This time, I want you to listen to me," said Garz very seriously. "Don't ever come back, alright?"

Erde nodded and bid Garz farewell. He continued down the street, pausing to look over his shoulder. Garz had disappeared once again. Erde wondered if Heidi and Fueur's souls would remain trapped in Furcht, but he pushed those thoughts out of his mind for now. That was something to pray upon later.

The swordsman opened the rusty gate and walked down the steps towards the mountain path leading home. He walked through the fog and out of Furcht. The entire road home, he did not look back once.

Epilogue

The man looked at the bare stone wall and ran his hand over it. The door was no more, opening only to rock. He laughed quietly, then walked up the staircase, away from the skeletal hands that had pulled him into the Necropolis so many years ago. He had not aged a day, but he had many years less to live after his dealings with the giant.

It was a bright morning, the first time he had seen the real sun in so long. He removed his left gauntlet and bathed his pale hand in the light. It felt natural; true warmth. A feeling he had long forgotten. There were so many things about the real world that he missed. Perhaps he would try food next? He could not remember the taste of bread or the feeling of drinking a fine, red wine.

He walked through the city, taking in the sights

that he knew so well, yet they differed in the real world. It was a strange feeling, not having to look out for the roaming ghouls. It was pleasant even though ghouls had become such a minor nuisance that he barely noticed them in recent years. He had grown powerful, far more so than any being that had ever stepped foot in Furcht.

Throughout his time in the accursed land of the unaging, many people had come and gone. Many had died in that wretched place while he survived. It was a bittersweet moment to finally be free, but the Necropolis was collapsing. That world had ended and it was time to return to reality at last.

Xantem's soul had been vanquished and no more lives needed to be sacrificed to leave, for the doorway was only an exit. Not that it mattered much, as the man had been the last living being remaining there. Now there was only the undead, trapped eternally in limbo. The souls of their once-living selves had departed to the world beyond, freed from the necromancy that held them to the Outer World.

The man had decided that it was finally his time. Everybody he knew was long gone, but he wondered if any of the lucky survivors had ever written about their escapades in the city. Maybe there were even tales of his own adventures? Perhaps he would seek out the Grand Library of Kalmere? Just to satisfy his curiosity. Well, he would seek it out if it was still there. Was Kalmere even called Kalmere anymore or was it a new nation entirely?

So much had changed, but he would have to see for himself what still remained. The Dusk Era had ended and those who hid in Furcht to escape the eclipse and the awakening of the Sleeping Ones told him the most dreadful tales, but the world looked decidedly normal. The worst must have come and gone.

The man in the golden armour, wielding his mace, walked towards the rusty gate. He looked to his right and spotted the ruins of the guardhouse. It was in remarkably worse condition than the one in the false Furcht. He remembered his first time here. How the old guard had warned him that no good would come of entering the Necropolis. The man knew now that he should have listened, but his sacrifices had made it so that no more sacrifices to the door would need to be made ever again. He had many regrets, but at least some good came from his mistake.

He walked down the steps and towards the mountain path, finding it overgrown. It was not much of a path, but it was the best there was. He wondered how many years ago the man who donned the black skull armour had walked this way. Many decades? A century? Counting had started to seem pointless. Perhaps, after the library, he would try to find the man's descendants and see if he ever made it home and reunited with his children. What was his name again? Art? Earth? Erde? Yes, that was it. Erde of Olfen.

The man had always been fond of that mercenary, even though they had only known each other for a couple of days. In the days since, the mercenary's two friends had regaled him with stories of their adventures from when their band was whole. Those friends were long gone from the Necropolis too. Not even Leer remained, the library now an abandoned temple of dust. No matter, the real library would be here in the Outer World, the knowledge kept safe by the departed bibliographers.

As he reminisced, the man's helmet rotated to a smiling face and he continued walking, leaving Furcht behind forever. A city in ruins with a sad history that was finally allowed to die.

Other Books by Jordan Allen

Mutagenesis: The New World (2021)

A post-apocalyptic sci-fi novel set in Texas decades after hordes of mutants wiped out civilisation. It's a tale of survival, adventure and coming to terms with misfortune.

Hollow Kingdom (2023)

The first book in the dark fantasy setting of the Hollow Realms. A sword and sorcery tale of a prince trying to reclaim his kingdom and solve the mystery of his father and brother's fates.

www.ingramcontent.com/pod-product-compliance
Lightning Source LLC
Chambersburg PA
CBHW071344170626
46811CB00003B/981